"Would You Quit The Casanova Routine Already?"

Carter observed her through narrowed eyes. "You think I'm trying to put the moves on you?"

Phoebe arched a brow and aimed for sarcasm. "Aren't you? The question is why?"

His jaw shifted and then he rocked back on his heels and shoved his hands in his pockets. "I'm curious. Aren't you?"

"About what?" she asked, even though she suspected she knew the answer.

"Whether it would be as good between us as it used to be."

Her stomach dropped to her shoes. Yes, the thought had crossed her mind a time or ten since making the decision to seek him out, but she had no intention of satisfying her curiosity. The last time she had he'd stolen her heart and shattered it into tiny, irreparable fragments.

She forced a casual shrug and lied through her teeth. "Not really. Now, if you don't mind, the picture."

Dear Reader,

Thank you for choosing Silhouette Desire, where this month we have six fabulous novels for you to enjoy. We start things off with *Estate Affair* by Sara Orwig, the latest installment of the continuing DYNASTIES: THE ASHTONS series. In this upstairs/downstairs-themed story, the Ashtons' maid falls for an Ashton son and all sorts of scandal follows. And in Maureen Child's *Whatever Reilly Wants…*, the second title in the THREE-WAY WAGER series, a sexy marine gets an unexpected surprise when he falls for his suddenly transformed gal pal.

Susan Crosby concludes her BEHIND CLOSED DOORS series with *Secrets of Paternity*. The secret baby in this book just happens to be eighteen years old…. Hmm, there's quite the story behind that revelation. The wonderful Emilie Rose presents *Scandalous Passion,* a sultry tale of a woman desperate to get back some steamy photos from her past lover. Of course, he has a price for returning those pictures, but it's not money he's after. *The Sultan's Bed,* by Laura Wright, continues the tales of her sheikh heroes with an enigmatic male who is searching for his missing sister and finds a startling attraction to her lovely neighbor. And finally, what was supposed to be just an elevator ride turns into a very passionate encounter, in *Blame It on the Blackout* by Heidi Betts.

Sit back and enjoy all of the smart, sensual stories Silhouette Desire has to offer.

Happy reading,

Melissa Jeglinski

Melissa Jeglinski
Senior Editor
Silhouette Desire

Please address questions and book requests to:
Silhouette Reader Service
U.S.: 3010 Walden Ave., P.O. Box 1325, Buffalo, NY 14269
Canadian: P.O. Box 609, Fort Erie, Ont. L2A 5X3

Scandalous Passion

Emilie Rose

Published by Silhouette Books
America's Publisher of Contemporary Romance

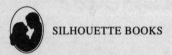 SILHOUETTE BOOKS

ISBN 0-373-76660-2

SCANDALOUS PASSION

Copyright © 2005 by Emilie Rose Cunningham

This edition published by arrangement with Harlequin Books S.A.

Visit Silhouette Books at www.eHarlequin.com

Printed in U.S.A.

Books by Emilie Rose

Silhouette Desire

Expecting Brand's Baby #1463
The Cowboy's Baby Bargain #1511
The Cowboy's Million-Dollar Secret #1542
A Passionate Proposal #1578
Forbidden Passion #1624
Breathless Passion #1635
Scandalous Passion #1660

EMILIE ROSE

lives in North Carolina with her college sweetheart husband and four sons. This bestselling author's love for romance novels developed when she was twelve years old and her mother hid them under sofa cushions each time Emilie entered the room. Emilie grew up riding and showing horses. She's a devoted baseball mom during the season and can usually be found in the bleachers watching one of her sons play. Her hobbies include quilting, cooking (especially cheesecake) and anything cowboy. Her favorite TV shows include Discovery Channel's medical programs, *ER* and *CSI*. Emilie's a country music fan because there's an entire book in nearly every song.

Emilie loves to hear from her readers and can be reached at P.O. Box 20145, Raleigh, NC, 27619 or at www.EmilieRose.com.

My thanks to the staff of the Shriners Hospital for Children in Greenville, South Carolina. I've never encountered a more generous group of individuals.

One

Clear the skeletons from your closet before your grandfather declares his presidential candidacy or the press will do it for you.

Phoebe Lancaster Drew smoothed damp palms over her most flattering navy suit and marched up the curving brick sidewalk with her grandfather's campaign manager's words echoing in her head.

It was rather pathetic really that the only skeletons in Phoebe's closet were a few private pictures taken twelve years ago. Excluding those nine exhilarating months, she'd behaved like a proper Southern belle her entire life, devoting her time to her family, worthy causes and, lately, her career. But oh, those months…

Her heart beat a little faster and her nerves coiled tighter as she inspected the elegant brick home. Had the university alumni association given her the correct address? A single man had no reason to choose a home with a huge yard in this quiet old neighborhood…unless he'd married and had children. She took a bracing breath, pressed the doorbell with one hand and covered her anxious stomach with the other.

Children. She and Carter Jones had once planned to have a family together.

Well, she stood a little straighter, if he'd found a woman to give him the home and family he'd always craved, she would be happy for him. But the prickle of discomfort between Phoebe's shoulder blades belied her words.

When no one responded to the doorbell, Phoebe leaned closer to peer through the stained-glass upper portion of the door. Discerning no movement inside, she rang the bell again and huffed in frustration. The sweet scent of the red and white petunias cascading from nearby urns filled her nostrils.

She had limited time to accomplish her task, and showing up unannounced on a Saturday afternoon in late May was risky, but she hadn't dared make her odd request via phone or take a chance on the photos getting lost in the mail.

Her grandfather planned to declare his candidacy in a matter of weeks, an action that would unleash the bloodhounds of the press on everyone connected to the senior senator from North Carolina. Phoebe would be a prime target because she'd served as his hostess since her grandmother's death, and she would be expected to continue in that role if her grandfather made it to the White House. She was also his chief speechwriter.

The sound of splashing caught her attention. Was there a pool behind the house? She made her way down the sidewalk and around the perimeter of the house, past fragrant gardenia bushes in full bloom and an open garage housing a black Saleen Mustang convertible. Her brows lifted. Carter driving a high-powered muscle car? The idea wouldn't mesh with the image of the tall, gangly computer nerd she'd loved to distraction during her first semester of college.

A military brat and a senator's granddaughter, they'd been an unlikely pair…just like her parents. And, like her parents, there hadn't been a happy ending for Phoebe and Carter. Her parents had given up everything—including her—for love and they'd died in each other's arms while chasing their dreams.

A large rectangular pool covered only a fraction of the expansive backyard. A single swimmer sliced a straight line through the sparkling water with swift, efficient strokes. Phoebe's stomach flip-flopped. Was it Carter? He reached the far end, executed an under-water turn and headed in her direction. Her mouth dried. *Get it done, Phoebe.*

Hoping this tanned man was indeed Carter and not a dark-haired stranger, she crossed the patio on trembling legs to wait on the concrete apron surrounding the pool. As he approached, Phoebe noticed the muscles roping his shoulders, arms and back, and the black barbed-wire tattoo circling his thick left bicep. She exhaled and relaxed her taut muscles. The mystery man couldn't be Carter, but he might know where she could find her former lover.

She knelt beside the pool's edge to get his attention, but before she could call out he erupted in a cascade of water and caught her ankle with his long fingers. Startled, Phoebe screamed and fell back on her bottom. She would have scrambled away, but his big hand held her in a vise grip.

The sapphire-blue eyes boring into hers looked achingly familiar as did the lush lips and sharply angled jaw. But those wide shoulders…those bulging biceps…that *tattoo*… Her mouth fell open. This couldn't be Carter Jones. Could it?

"Carter?" Her voice cracked.

"Phoebe?" He sounded as surprised as she was.

My God, what had happened to him? He'd turned into—
she swallowed hard—*beefcake*. Blinking, she shook her head.
Dampness seeped through her clothing, cooling her hot skin.
She'd landed in a puddle. Her silk skirt would be ruined. She
clambered to her feet as gracefully as she could given the fact
that her knees had about as much strength as overcooked lin-
guini and her stomach resided in her leather pumps. She
sighed in relief when he released her, but the ring of his damp
fingers remained imprinted on her skin.

"Why did you grab me like that?"

"I thought you were one of my neighbors. They're notorious
for their lousy practical jokes." Carter heaved himself from the
pool in an act of rippling muscles and sheer intimidating size.
Phoebe staggered back a few steps and stared in disbelief at the
Adonis standing in front of her. She hadn't forgotten Carter's
impressive height, but he was broader now—*much broader*—
than the lanky boy she'd held in her arms. He took up an overwhelming amount of space on the sun-drenched patio.

Stunned by the changes in him, she let her gaze follow the
water streaming from the cords of his neck to his expansive,
muscular shoulders and chest, his six-pack abs and shallow
navel. He had more chest hair now. Dark whorls spattered his
pectorals, narrowing into a thin line that led to brief navy
swimming trunks riding low on his narrow hips. Like the rest
of him, his legs were well-developed. A series of pink scars
marred his left knee, but other than that, the man was perfec-
tion personified wrapped in wet, golden-brown skin.

Heat filled her belly and her face. *Oh my.* She closed her
mouth and met his amused gaze.

"I—I—" For heaven's sake, she manipulated words by
trade, but sitting behind a desk and composing moving political speeches was a far cry from coming up with intelligent
off-the-cuff remarks when faced with…*this*.

"You're going to give me a complex about what a scrawny geek I used to be if you keep staring."

Ashamed of her gawking, she stammered, "Y-you've certainly…built up some muscles."

His eyes hardened and his lips flattened. "The Marine Corps will do that to you."

"Marines? You're a Marine?" She scrambled to make sense of the news. Carter had spent his childhood following his career-officer father around the world. He'd claimed he hated the vagabond military life and that he'd wanted nothing more than to set down roots. *With her.*

A shadow crossed his face. "Not anymore. What can I do for you, Ms. Drew?"

"Lancaster Drew," she corrected automatically. He still spoke in the soft, rumbling baritone she remembered, but his voice now carried an unmistakable air of authority and confidence.

"Right. Let's not forget your ties to the venerated Senator Lancaster." His bitterness couldn't have been clearer.

"I, uh…" *Can't think with all that taut skin on display. Wow, he looks amazing.*

Don't stare, Phoebe. Her grandmother's scold rang in her ears.

Phoebe spotted a towel on a nearby chair, picked it up and offered it to Carter. He didn't take the hint to cover up, but merely swiped the water from his hair and face, then draped the fabric around his neck. A dark lock flopped over his forehead and her fingers itched to sweep it back as she'd done so many times.

Struggling to regain a smidgeon of composure, Phoebe averted her gaze and studied the deep, covered porch on his two-story home. Hanging baskets of bright flowers and a hummingbird feeder dangled from the eaves, and she recalled the urns of flowers out front, as well. Carter very likely had a wife. Her stomach burned.

Phoebe took a peek at his ring finger and found it bare, but that didn't necessarily mean anything since some men didn't wear rings. Besides, rekindling their romance *wasn't* why she was here.

Resolved to get this encounter over with as quickly as possible, she focused on her task, gathered her courage and met his hard gaze. "I wanted to talk to you about the past. Specifically, our past and our...pictures."

His eyes narrowed. "What pictures?"

Her cheeks warmed. Very conscious of the wet silk clinging to her bottom, she shifted on her feet. "You know which pictures. The *intimate* ones," she added the last in a whisper even though there was no one around to hear. They had the additional privacy of thick magnolia trees forming a natural screen between the lawn and the woodland beyond.

Laughter glinted in Carter's eyes and one corner of his mouth tipped up in a naughty smile, puncturing his cheek with a dimple. He did a little inspecting of his own and Phoebe cringed inwardly. She hadn't improved with age the way he had. In fact most of the ten pounds she'd gained since college had settled below her waist.

"Ah, *those* pictures."

Why did her insides go all fizzy like a shaken bottle of champagne when he looked at her that way? "Do you still have them?"

"Why?" He folded his arms over his bulging pectorals. His hard nipples pointed at her. The memory of how those tiny pebbles had felt against her tongue blindsided her. Heat coursed through her veins.

The man had a body to die for, but the tattoo drew her gaze like an ice-cream truck draws children. "That had to hurt."

She wanted to slap a hand over her wayward mouth, but she didn't. Dear heaven, had she regressed to that awkward girl-with-her-first-crush bumbling? Where was her poise, her professional *politically correct* demeanor?

"If it did, I was too drunk to notice." More bitterness.

Carter hadn't been a drinker when they were together, but then, Phoebe hadn't been old enough to drink legally back then. She'd been barely eighteen when they'd met. He'd been twenty-one and a senior. "Do you have the pictures?"

"Maybe. Why?" he repeated. His poker face held no clue to his thoughts.

What had happened to the guy he used to be? Her friend. Her lover. The one person she could talk to for hours? Everything about him seemed harder: his body, his voice and his eyes. She curled her fingers in frustration and searched for the words to complete her task.

"I'd like to have them—"

"Missing me?" His grin reappeared, dimpling both cheeks this time.

"—and the negatives," she continued as if he hadn't interrupted. Her heart was going to pound itself to mush if he didn't stop smiling that way. That knowing sparkle in his eyes used to mean one, or both, of them would be naked within seconds, and once they were naked…

She plucked at her silk blouse, separating it from her suddenly damp skin. Moisture pooled between her thighs. *Shameful.* Why couldn't she catch her breath? She blamed it on the Carolina heat and humidity, and then nearly laughed out loud. Talk about putting a political spin on a situation…

All traces of humor faded from his expression. "Do you plan to show the pictures around and tell everybody about the time you went slumming?"

Embarrassment licked through her. "It wasn't slumming,

Carter. My grandfather is about to announce his presidential candidacy. In the wrong hands those pictures could jeopardize his campaign."

"So this is about your grandfather's career again?" His clipped words and ice-chip eyes revealed his anger.

Carter had never understood how much she owed her grandparents for taking her in after her parents had abandoned her—a fact he'd proven when he asked her to choose between him and her grandfather twelve years ago.

"It's also about mine. I'm his speech writer. I'd like to destroy the pictures. We were young and rash and—"

"No." He stepped around her, heading for the house in long strides.

Oh, my. His back side was just as firm and impressive as his front side. The muscles rippling in the triangular *V* of his back as he dried himself muddled her thoughts so badly she almost missed his refusal. "What do you mean, *no?*"

"No, you can't have the pictures," he called over his shoulder without slowing.

She hurried after him. "Surely your wife doesn't like you having pictures of another woman in the house."

He stopped and turned so abruptly she bumped into him. Her palms landed on the bare, hot skin of his chest. Before she could withdraw, he caught her wrists, holding her captive. His gaze ensnared hers just as surely as he'd trapped her hands against his body. His nipples bored into her palms. Her heart leaped to her throat and her breath stalled in her lungs.

"I'm not married," he said in that low, husky voice that used to melt her like butter in a hot skillet. "You?"

"N-no." That was *not* relief sweeping through her system. And surely the weakness in her knees could be attributed to missing breakfast and lunch rather than the thud of his heart and the warmth of his skin beneath her hands. She tugged and he released her. "You live in this huge house alone?"

"Yeah. Got a deal on it. It needed work. I'm restoring it."

"It's lovely." Her palms tingled.

"It's even better inside."

The unspoken invitation—with the arch of a challenging eyebrow thrown in—sent alarm racing through her. She broke away from his mesmerizing gaze and glanced at her watch. "I'm a bit pressed for time. Could you please hand over the pictures and negatives, and I'll get out of your way. I'll wait here."

His chin set in a stubborn line. "Come inside and we'll discuss it."

She wanted to howl in frustration, but of course, she'd never do that. The senior senator's granddaughter would never be so crass as to stamp her feet or to publicly show her displeasure. *Never let them see you sweat,* her grandfather had cautioned on more than one occasion. And never, ever, say words you can't take back. She'd learned the hard way.

"Carter, let's not take a trip down memory lane. It would serve no purpose."

"Except to humor me—the one with the pictures." Did she imagine the flash of anger in his eyes or the sarcastic twist of his lips? He tugged the towel from around his neck and dried his hips and legs. Muscles rippled with every move. In her dark-suit-and-tasteful-necktie world she didn't get much exposure to sleek, tanned skin. Her mouth dried and her pulse couldn't seem to find its regular rhythm.

"So you do have them?"

"Yep." He climbed the steps of his porch and held open the door. Phoebe paused. She could refuse his invitation and *perhaps* never see the pictures again. No, the possible peril was too great. She had to stick with her agenda to recover and destroy the evidence of her shameful past. Lifting her chin, she swept up the stairs and into his sunny breakfast area. She felt his eyes on her backside as she passed and wished she could suck it in the way she sucked in her tummy.

"I got you wet. Sorry. Want me to toss your skirt in the dryer?"

She studied him. Did he intend the double entendre? And did he honestly expect her to hand over her skirt? "No, it's silk. It has to be line dried."

"I can loan you some shorts and we'll hang your skirt out on the deck."

She'd borrowed his clothing in the past, but she couldn't imagine doing so today. She wasn't the casual type any longer. Image was everything in politics. Besides, she didn't intend to be here long enough for the fabric to dry. "No, thank you."

"Have a seat." He jabbed a finger toward the kitchen table. "A wet butt won't hurt the chairs. I'll be back in a minute."

Carter disappeared into what looked like the laundry room at the opposite end of the kitchen, but he didn't close the door. Phoebe could hear him moving around and her imagination rioted at the thought of him stripping off his snug racing trunks, revealing his taut buttocks and the part of him she'd spent so much time exploring. They'd shared a lot of hasty mutual stripping in their past, first in his dorm room and then at out-of-the-way hotels and on deserted back roads once she'd changed universities.

With her pulse racing, Phoebe sank into a chair at the wrought-iron glass-topped table, averted her eyes from the open door and battled an urge to fan her hot face. She hadn't expected to still find Carter attractive, but the days of giving her heart or her body to a man were over. Carter had been her first lover, but he hadn't been in love with her or he wouldn't have broken her heart. She'd fooled herself once and had no intention of repeating the painful mistake of confusing sexual desire with love ever again.

* * *

Of all the people Carter Jones had expected to see standing beside his pool, Phoebe Lancaster Drew didn't make the list.

Carter ripped off his trunks and swore as the abrupt movement sent a sharp stabbing pain up his thigh. It had been three and a half years since the accident that had ended his military career, and for the most part he was pain-free unless he did something stupid. He'd expected the wavering shadow at the pool edge to be one of his neighbors or one of his ex-Marine buddies, although the pity visits had thinned out since his new company had taken off. Thank God.

He yanked on a pair of ragged cut-off shorts and a tank top. No need to dress to impress the senator's granddaughter. She'd written him off as her dirty secret years ago. Good enough to screw, but not to marry.

What had happened to the girl he'd fallen for? Had she even existed outside his imagination? Probably not.

Phoebe's conservative suit and tightly twisted-up sable hair, combined with a ramrod-straight spine reminded him of the day he'd surprised her at her grandfather's Washington, D.C., home—the day the blinders had fallen away from Carter's eyes and his world had collapsed. The day he'd discovered Phoebe didn't love him.

His parents had been coming stateside for his university graduation, and he'd wanted them to meet his future wife, but Phoebe hadn't been happy to see Carter on her grandfather's doorstep. She'd acted as if she couldn't get him out of the house fast enough. When her grandfather had arrived, she'd shown her true colors by introducing him to the senator not as her lover or her fiancé, but as *a classmate*, for crissake. Her refusal to come with him to meet his parents combined with the lukewarm intro to the senator had said it all. They had no future together. He'd been nothing but a toy to Phoebe Lancaster Drew. Unimportant. Temporary. Expendable.

And now Phoebe wanted to erase what had happened between them twelve years ago. He ground his teeth and struggled to tamp down his anger. Those photographs were proof that the senator's beautiful granddaughter had done the dirty with a mongrel military brat. Hell, if it wasn't for the pictures, Carter probably wouldn't believe the two of them had once been as close as lovers can be. He'd made the mistake of believing their hearts had been as connected as their bodies, but that was the gullibility of youth and inexperience for you.

He padded barefoot into the kitchen, extracted two glasses from the cabinet, then pulled a pitcher of tea from the refrigerator. He carried his load to the table, poured and slid a glass in her direction. She looked so damned rigid he wanted to bark, "At ease."

But helping Phoebe relax wasn't his job. Not anymore.

Settling across from her, he nodded at her murmured thanks and leaned back in his chair. Her light floral scent—the same perfume she'd worn twelve years ago—hit him with a C-130 military transport plane full of memories. He used to know every pulse point she anointed with the stuff *intimately*. He swigged his drink to ease the dryness in his mouth and assessed the changes in Phoebe over the rim of his glass.

She was still a beauty with her dark hair and changeable hazel-green eyes, but the fire and excitement had faded from those eyes and tension flattened the lush curve of her mouth. She looked too poised and proper, too much like a storefront mannequin for his tastes. It was almost as if someone had sucked the life right out of her, and that saddened him.

Not your problem, Jones.

"Are you happy being your grandfather's sidekick?"

She blinked at his question. "As opposed to what?"

"Working at a museum or teaching at the university."

She sucked in a sharp breath, apparently surprised he remembered her long-ago plans. He wished he could forget those nine months and the pain of discovering he'd never be good enough for Phoebe Lancaster Drew. Despite the fact that he was now worth millions, Carter Jones could never be a part of her old-moneyed, politically connected world.

"I'll have time for that later." She fingered her glass instead of meeting his gaze. The thick line of her lashes cast shadows on her smooth cheeks.

"And what about the family you once claimed to crave? Say granddad gets elected and possibly even reelected, although he's pretty old for a second term. You're thirty. If you wait for Wilton Lancaster to retire, you'll be pushing forty before you get started."

He hated the polite and insincere politician's smile curving her lips. It did nothing to eradicate the sadness in her eyes. "I've decided to focus on my career. And my grandfather will be seventy when he's inaugurated. He's eager to break Reagan's record of sixty-nine. Given that Granddad is in excellent health and is very active and mentally acute, a second term isn't out of the question."

"He's been in office more than thirty years. He ought to retire." *And give someone more open-minded a chance.* But Carter kept the last to himself.

Her long fingers curled around the glass. "What are you doing with yourself these days, Carter?"

He sipped and nodded, silently acknowledging her change of topic. She wanted chitchat? He could do chitchat. "Computers. What else?"

They'd met when he'd been assigned to tutor her in computer science during college. She'd been the first female he'd met whose eyes hadn't glazed over when he nervously rambled on about motherboards, memory chips and hard drives. And she hadn't laughed at him when he'd lost track of his words each time they'd accidentally brushed against each other.

"What exactly do you do with them?"

"I'm a cyber-cop." The surprise arching her eyebrows grated on his nerves. Had she, like his father, expected him to amount to nothing? Probably. His father had always claimed Carter's infatuation with computers would lead nowhere. Well, he'd proven good ol' Dad wrong, hadn't he?

"You investigate computer crimes?"

"Got it in one."

"You must be good." And then she flushed as if she realized that wasn't exactly a politically correct comment. Jeez, somebody needed to loosen her up. Her candid comments had been only one of the things he used to love about her.

"I own my company, but computers aren't the only thing I'm good at." He flashed a carnal grin and watched another wave of peach spread from her neck over her cheeks. Teasing Phoebe had always been fun, and now that she seemed determined to ignore the passion that had once flowed between them, he took perverse pleasure in getting a rise out of her.

He set down his glass and laced his fingers over his abs. "Why should I give you the pictures, Phoebe?"

The taste of her name on his tongue made him think of hot nights and tangled sheets, of quickies in the car or anywhere else they could grab a moment's privacy vertically, horizontally or otherwise. His pulse quickened. His inability to control his response only increased his anger. Why, dammit, did she still rev his motor? She'd been his first lover, but she hadn't been his last. He'd been a slow starter, but he'd made up for lost time. There had been plenty of willing women, sweaty sex and tussles between the sheets since.

"I need to be certain they won't turn up in the press."

The insult raised his blood pressure. "You think I'd sell our pictures to the highest bidder?"

He practically could see her weighing her words. "Perhaps not, but someone else could get their hands on them and—"

"It won't happen. The pictures are under lock and key. They have been since we said goodbye. If I didn't sell them then, when I was seriously pis—peeved with you, I'm not likely to now."

She wet her lips—one slick swipe of her pink tongue— and fire flickered behind his zipper. Phoebe had once had an amazingly talented mouth. She'd perfected her technique on him, and she'd allowed him the pleasure of returning the favor.

"Carter, please, let me have the pictures."

He rocked back in his chair and steepled his hands. Tapping his bottom lip with one finger, he pretended to consider her request, but there was no way in hell he'd casually hand over the pictures for her to shred. He didn't look at them often, hadn't seen them since he'd moved into this house three years ago, in fact, but they represented the first time in his life when he hadn't felt like a failure. Phoebe's betrayal had cut deep and made him feel like a shameful dirty secret, but for a while she'd made him feel like a king.

A spark of an idea began to form. He'd been an untried boy twelve years ago when he and Phoebe lost their virginity together. Afterward they'd explored the boundaries of their newfound sexuality and shared some amazingly uninhibited sex. He hadn't met a woman since who could ignite him to such a fever pitch or coax him into the unknown with nothing more than a naughty twinkle in her eyes. No woman in the past twelve years had pushed him beyond his rigidly imposed self-control.

Surely his memories of their time together had exaggerated her potency? No way could this buttoned-up, every-hair-in-place woman have the same power over the experienced man he'd become that she'd held over the wet-behind-the-ears boy he'd been. So he'd slake his curiosity and then kiss her goodbye. In the process, maybe he could loosen up Phoebe and teach her a lesson at the same time. Ms. Phoebe *Lancaster* Drew needed to learn how it felt to be used and tossed aside.

Vengeance could indeed be sweet. And sexually satisfying.

Carter rolled the cool glass in his palms when what he really wanted to do was to cup Phoebe's rigid jaw and test the texture of her skin. "I'll make you a deal."

Her grip on the glass tightened and her eyes narrowed suspiciously. "What kind of deal?"

"Go out with me and I'll give you the pictures. Let's say, one picture for each date. There are roughly a dozen photos."

Her laugh sounded choked. "You're joking, of course."

He held her gaze, noting the angry gold flecks sparkling in the green of her irises, but said nothing.

"Why?"

He shrugged one shoulder and set down his tea. "Because I said so."

She rolled her eyes. "That's so juvenile."

"No dates. No pictures. No negotiation."

Her pale-pink manicured nails pressed dents into her palms. "That's blackmail."

"So sue me. But then, of course, the pictures would become evidence and public knowledge." He abruptly rocked forward and covered her fists with his hands. He stroked the satiny skin inside her wrists with his thumbs, and her pulse leaped beneath his touch. His echoed the rapid beat.

"Remember how much fun we used to have, Phoebe?"

She jerked her hands free, but he didn't miss the irregularity of her breathing or the pulse fluttering at the base of her throat. It all boiled down to how badly she wanted those pictures.

She lifted her chin. "I won't sleep with you."

A smile of anticipation tugged his lips. He'd learned a lot about women in the past decade—specifically, how to recognize when one found him attractive. And Phoebe had definitely been checking him out. Not only would she have sex with him, he planned to make her beg for it. "I didn't ask you to, but I appreciate you making your views clear up front so I don't get my hopes—*or anything else*—up."

Her cheeks turned crimson and she shifted in her seat. "One date per picture. I get to choose which picture."

He mashed his lips together. "No deal. I set up the dates. I choose the pictures."

The muscle in her jaw flexed as she clenched her teeth. "I want to see them."

Gotcha. He grinned so hard his cheek muscles ached.

"Do you, now?" he asked in a teasing lilt and could practically hear her molars grinding in response.

"I want proof that you still have them."

He rose and gestured toward the den. "They're in my bedroom."

She remained seated. "Is that your version of 'Come and see my etchings'?"

For the first time in a long time he couldn't stop smiling. "I don't have etchings. I have Kodak moments."

She looked ready to explode. Her nose inched higher. "Who else has seen them?"

He scowled. Another insult. "You think I'd kiss and tell?"

She primly folded her hands in her lap. "Get the pictures, Carter. I'll wait here."

He didn't call her a coward, but he let his eyes say it for him. Her spine stiffened. Message received.

"Make yourself comfortable. I'll be right back."

Carter glanced at his waterproof watch as he crossed the den. Operation Seduction under way at 1700 hours.

Let the games begin.

Two

Phoebe put her head in her hands. She had to be out of her mind to agree to Carter's ridiculous terms. Could she grab the photos and run? Hardly. Carter might have been a geek twelve years ago, but he looked to be in peak physical condition now. He'd outrun her. Besides, he could always print more pictures from the negatives. She needed the pictures *and* the negatives.

Her grandfather had always said that if you couldn't change your opponent's mind, then you had to wear him down. So Phoebe decided she'd play Carter's childish game. As luck would have it, her grandfather would be at his Bald Head Island retreat for the next month preparing campaign strategies and meeting with his advisers. She'd stayed behind to research his most likely opponents and to look for good quotes for his next speech. Odds were that she could probably recover the pictures without having to explain her whereabouts.

As far as Carter's abundant sex appeal went, she hadn't made it to the age of thirty without learning how to handle her physical needs. Messy, complicated relationships were not required. Resisting him wouldn't be easy, but it was within her capabilities. All she had to do was to focus and get to know her opponent—another of her grandfather's maxims.

From her seat at the table Phoebe examined Carter's house, looking for clues to the man he'd become. In college he'd claimed he wanted a place to put down the roots his childhood hadn't permitted. He'd certainly achieved that goal. Sunlight flooded his kitchen, illuminating very traditional oak cabinets and gleaming hardwood floors. Wooden beams supported the vaulted ceiling of the spacious den to her right, and a huge brick fireplace flanked by tall windows covered most of the outside wall. The leather sofa and chairs looked masculine and expensive, but the room begged for color and softness, for a woman's touch.

The lack of decorative elements inside led Phoebe to believe Carter didn't have a woman in his life. But the flowers surrounding his porches and the hummingbird feeder contradicted the lonely bachelor theory. Carter had never been a birds-and-blooms kind of guy. She didn't think he'd become one. And she couldn't imagine a man with his sex appeal being alone. So who was the woman in his life? Or did he keep more than one on a string?

Never mind. It didn't matter. This was a business transaction not a courtship. A barter agreement. Nothing more. She had to uncover his true motive. What did he want in exchange for the pictures? She didn't believe for one minute that all he wanted was the pleasure of her company.

Carter reappeared with the pictures fanned out in his fingers like playing cards, the backs facing Phoebe. He looked mouthwateringly gorgeous with his shoulder and arm muscles displayed like a handsome hunk calendar model's. And that tattoo… She couldn't believe it turned her on. Did he have more? Where? Her pulse quickened.

Your curiosity will bring you nothing but trouble, Phoebe Lancaster Drew, her grandmother's voice, which often doubled as Phoebe's conscience, chided. And her grandmother always had been right. Besides, Phoebe had seen most of Carter in his swimsuit. If he had tattoos beneath the brief trunks, she wouldn't be seeing them.

She didn't want to look at the pictures, didn't want to be reminded of how deeply she'd trusted Carter or how unimportant she'd been to him, but for all she knew he could be bluffing. She held out her hand. He thumped the rectangles into a neat stack and passed them to her. The brush of his fingertips against her palm forced the air from her lungs. Phoebe averted her gaze from his and found herself looking at the worn denim to the left of Carter's zipper. A jolt of energy shot through her. She gulped. Looking at the pictures hadn't left him unaffected. Well—she squared her shoulders—*she* would have more control over her baser instincts.

Bracing herself, she turned the rectangles over. Her heart skipped a beat and her hand wobbled. The picture on top of the stack was probably the most innocent of all the photos they'd taken with Carter's old camera set on a timer. Carter stood straight, tall and completely nude with his back to the camera. Phoebe couldn't help contrasting the lanky frame in the photograph with the muscle-packed body in front of her. She'd been standing in front of him, completely concealed from the camera by his body except for her forearms and hands. She'd wrapped her arms around his waist to cup his buttocks. Those pale hands could have belonged to anyone except for the identifying heirloom signet ring on her right ring finger—the same ring she wore every day of her life.

Phoebe curled her fist by her side, but it was no use trying to hide the ring. Heat swept through her as she remembered how his thick erection had burned against her stomach, her nipples had scraped his bare chest and how his own hands had cupped her bottom. Moments after the shutter clicked he'd lifted her, filled her with one deep stroke, and loved her until they'd both collapsed on the floor, too weak to move until the sound of his roommate's key grating in the lock had sent them scrambling for their clothing.

She'd loved Carter Jones beyond reason and this picture brought those feelings rushing back with a force she couldn't dam. Fast on the heels of the hot, fizzy arousal racing through her blood came pain—the pain of his desertion. He hadn't loved her enough.

She always lost the ones she loved. She'd been abandoned by her fun-loving parents when she was seven. They'd been killed in a rebel uprising in some godforsaken land six years later. The signet ring was the only memento she had of her mother. Her grandmother, who'd become Phoebe's surrogate mother, had passed away quickly and unexpectedly four months after Phoebe started at the university, and then Phoebe had lost Carter five months later.

Her grandfather was the only family Phoebe had left, and now it seemed her grandfather's approval hinged on her standing beside him in his presidential bid. Heaven only knew what would happen if these pictures leaked out and Phoebe's indiscretion tainted his campaign. Would he abandon her, too, or did he love her enough to forgive her for her wild and impetuous first love? It wasn't a chance she was willing to take.

"I'll buy them from you. How much do you want?"

"The pictures aren't for sale." His hard expression warned her not to waste time arguing.

Unable to bear looking through the rest of the photos,

Phoebe passed them back. "Then I want the negatives as a show of good faith."

"No can do, sugar. Not until the last date."

Sugar. Sweet to the taste and habit-forming. She closed her eyes against the memory of him looking up at her from between her legs with a smile slanting his damp lips as he uttered those words. She lifted her eyelids and met Carter's gaze. The watchful expression on his face told her he also remembered the often-repeated phrase and its context.

"I want your word that you won't show these pictures to anyone else."

"You have it," he replied without hesitation.

Phoebe bolstered her resistance. "When do we start?"

"Tomorrow. Where are you staying?"

"My grandfather's home in Raleigh."

"I'll pick you up at six."

"No." Alarm raced through her bloodstream. "That's not necessary. I'll meet you."

Carter's jaw turned to granite. "Still worried what Granddad will say if your former *classmate* turns up on your doorstep?"

He remembered the awkward introduction to her grandfather, but he hadn't waited around long enough for Phoebe to explain why she'd been so cautious. "He's out of town."

His lips curled in disgust. "Figures. I pick my dates up and I see them back to their door…unless they spend the night with me."

A nerve beneath her right eye twitched—a telltale sign of stress she'd never been able to conquer. "That will not be the case. I'll meet you here and then you can see me back to my *car* door."

His mouth set in a militant line and he looked ready to argue, but then he acquiesced with a sharp nod. "Fine. Six."

Her heart stuttered. One battle won, but certainly not the war. *Phoebe Lancaster Drew, what have you gotten yourself into?*

He'd expected Phoebe to chicken out. Instead she arrived thirty-three minutes early.

Carter lowered the dumbbell to the floor and wiped the sweat from his face with a towel. The slamming of his heart had nothing to do with his strenuous workout and everything to do with the slender woman striding up his front walk. The knowledge didn't please him.

It had been a bitch of a day—mainly because he couldn't keep his mind off tonight. Jes, his executive assistant, had threatened to quit if Carter didn't stop barking commands. Jes had claimed it was bad enough he was working on a Sunday to finish a last-minute proposal. Finally, Carter had left work and come home to take out his frustration on his free weights. He descended the stairs from his upstairs workout room and opened the door before Phoebe could ring the bell.

Her dark brows lifted as she inspected his sweaty workout tank and shorts. She tilted her head and firmed her mouth. "Am I overdressed?"

He checked out her tailored dress—a close twin to yesterday's stuffy and uptight suit. The navy-blue fabric gently draped her breasts, but it couldn't hide the pebbling of her nipples. Unfortunately the concealing garment skimmed past the curve of her hips to cover most of her long legs. Too bad Phoebe had first-class legs.

"You're early. I need to get ready."

"I allowed extra time for traffic but there wasn't any. Besides, the sooner we start, the sooner I can get home."

Her barb caught him like a sucker punch, but damn if he'd let it show. He hid his irritation by wiping his sweaty face with the towel and gesturing for her to come inside. "You want to look around while I shower and dress or do you want to wait for the guided tour?"

"Neither, thanks." She declined and insulted so politely Carter just shook his head.

"Give me ten minutes. There's iced tea in the fridge. Help yourself." He gestured toward the kitchen and then headed for the master suite.

Carter stripped and stepped under the shower spray, pondering how he could still find Phoebe attractive after all this time. Soaping his shoulders, he shrugged. Probably because they'd explored all kinds of uncharted territory with an uninhibited thirst for knowledge that he hadn't experienced since. Blood pooled in his groin and his heart pumped double-time at the mythological proportions of his memories. What better way to debunk that myth than by spending a month in her company? Then he'd find himself a sweet local gal, settle down and have kids.

Roots. That's what this old house was all about. He'd spent most of his life traveling the globe, and it was time to put down roots, to make his own history. Surely a family of his own would fill the void inside him? His parents didn't count since his dad was stationed halfway around the world and Carter rarely saw them.

He wanted a love like theirs—the kind that meant no sacrifice was too great. In all the years of their marriage, Carter had never heard his mother complain about any of the hellholes his father had dragged her through, and there'd been dozens of them. She'd packed and moved on command like a good military wife, happy to go anywhere as long as it meant staying by her husband's side. Even when she had to stay behind she'd been a pillar of strength, a rock he could rely on. At each new base she'd thrown herself into the wives clubs with enthusiasm.

As a shy kid, Carter hadn't made new friends as easily. He'd turned to books and cameras and, later, to computers. He'd been shy and tongue-tied around girls and hadn't made any real, lasting friendships until college. He and his college buddies Sawyer and Rick had remained tight until recently when both men had married and started families of their own, leaving Carter the odd man out once again. He hated being a fifth wheel.

He wanted a life partner, and as soon as he proved that his memories of Phoebe were nothing more than exaggerated fantasies, he'd find the right woman—a woman who wouldn't look down her straight, pedigreed nose at him or be ashamed to introduce him to her family. The timing was right. He had the home, and after three years of damned hard work, Cyber-Sniper was on solid footing.

Phoebe wasn't that woman. Hell, she hadn't even been able to look beyond the first photo in the stack he'd handed her yesterday. Was he such a repugnant part of her past?

He rinsed the shampoo from his hair, stepped out of the shower and dried off. After a quick shave, he pulled on a custom-tailored suit, shoved his feet into his Gucci loafers and headed for the kitchen and a little "hair of the dog that bit you."

Phoebe heard Carter return, but she couldn't look away from the picture of the adorable dark-haired, blue-eyed boy on Carter's refrigerator. Carter had said he wasn't married, but that didn't mean he didn't have an ex-wife and children somewhere. He was thirty-three and statistically likely to have married at least once by now.

"Is he yours?" Getting the words past the unexpected lump in her throat was harder than it should have been. Of course Carter would have children one day and they would not be hers. She'd buried those dreams long ago.

"No. J.C.—Joshua Carter—belongs to Sawyer Riggan. You remember my college roommate? He married a few years back. Sawyer and his wife Lynn are my neighbors. J.C.'s two years old, and he's my godson." Pride filled his voice.

"He's adorable." Phoebe turned from the picture and shock erased whatever she'd been about to say from her mind. Carter wore a charcoal-gray suit that fit his frame perfectly. His crisp white shirt accentuated his tanned face, and he'd knotted a sapphire-blue tie the exact shade of his eyes at his neck. A lock of damp dark hair fell over his forehead. He could have been any politician on Capitol Hill, only she'd never met a congressman this gorgeous.

His prosperous appearance threw her off balance and piqued her curiosity. Carter looked nothing like the rumpled, jeans-clad college student she used to know or the jock she'd encountered yesterday and again today when she'd arrived.

She blinked to clear the fog of unwanted attraction from her brain. Repeating past mistakes wasn't on the agenda. "You and Sawyer bought houses on the same street? You must have stayed close after school."

"Yeah. And Rick Faulkner and his wife own the third house on the street. Remember him?"

"The tall blonde?" She remembered Carter's two handsome friends, but she hadn't been interested in either of them back then. She'd been too busy losing herself in Carter's eyes, in his smile and, later, in his body. Unwelcome warmth settled low in her abdomen.

He nodded. "Want a drink? We have a few minutes before our reservation."

"No, thank you. As I said, I would really like to get home early tonight. I'm expecting a call from my grandfather."

His lips flat-lined. "Right. Let's go. I'll bring the car around front."

"There's no need, Carter. This isn't a real date. I can get into the car in the garage when you do."

A muscle in his jaw twitched, and then he jerked a nod. "Let me lock up."

He disappeared into the foyer and returned seconds later—long before Phoebe could come up with a way to convince him to hand over the pictures and cancel this outing. After opening the door leading from the kitchen to the garage, he activated the security keypad by the door. A custom-tailored suit, an alarm system and a sports car all added up to affluence.

He led Phoebe to his car and opened the door. Carefully avoiding his touch, she slid into the bucket seat and inhaled a subtle blend of leather and Carter's cologne—a costly designer fragrance unless she missed her guess. His company must be successful. Had money changed the man? And why did she care? Because Carter had never valued her for her old-moneyed family or her grandfather's clout. He'd seen *her*, not the senator's granddaughter. The men she'd met since were only interested in her connection to the most powerful senator in Washington—a lesson she'd learned the hard way.

Carter settled in the driver's seat. His large frame took up most of the interior and drained the oxygen from the enclosed space. How many times had they fogged up the windows making out in his old economy car or her sedate sedan twelve years ago? She shook off the memory.

"Where are we going?"

"A new restaurant." The car's powerful engine rumbled to life. At the touch of a button, the garage door lifted, letting in the evening light. Carter's hand nudged her knee as he reached for the gearshift. Phoebe moved her leg out of the danger zone, but not soon enough to prevent the tingle traveling upward. She pressed her knees together.

*Stick to the agenda, Phoebe. Twelve dates. No dalliance.
No broken promises. No broken heart.*

Carter's house was one of three stately older homes on the
secluded forest-surrounded street. "When and why did you
join the Marine Corps? I thought you hated that vagabond life."

"After graduation. For the job training."

He'd graduated days after they'd said goodbye. Had their
breakup caused him to have a change of heart about settling
down? He didn't elaborate as he took the winding road down-
hill with curve-hugging speed until he reached the stop sign
at the main thoroughfare.

"And now you're out," she prompted.

"Yes." The car shot forward into a break in traffic with a
burst of leashed power.

"Why not become a lifer like your father? He should be
way up there in rank now."

The bunching of his jaw muscle was his only response.

"Carter, you forced these outings. The least you can do is
converse politely."

He cut her a quick look. "My father has been promoted to
Lieutenant General. That's three stars. I received a medical
discharge after I blew out my knee on my last mission."

She remembered the scars. "I'm sorry."

"I'm not. It was time to get out of the military. I was in a
holding pattern that had nothing to do with where I wanted
to go with my life."

His reply hit a little too close to home. She shifted in her
seat. "Do you work with Sawyer? I remember the two of you
once talked about opening a company together."

"No. I fly solo."

She didn't think he referred only to business.

Minutes later Carter's car swept up the circular drive of a
stone castle-style structure complete with twin octagonal tur-

rets. A valet rushed to take his keys and another opened Phoebe's door just in time for Carter to hand her out. Carter's warm fingers wrapped around hers, sending a current of electricity up her arm. It always had been that way between them. She exhaled a pent-up breath when he released her, but her relief was short-lived when his palm settled against her spine. A shiver of awareness inched its way up her vertebrae.

She tightened her grip on her purse. "Wasn't this a private residence when we were students at the university?"

"The family fell on hard times and sold it. Old money surrenders to new. The current owner turned the estate into a restaurant with dancing. He wants to work up to hosting weddings, but for now you might want to tell the senator it's a good place for private parties."

Carter seemed to know an awful lot about the owner's plans. But Phoebe had no intention of dancing with Carter tonight or of telling her grandfather that she'd been on a date. The admission would lead to an inquisition and a discussion of the suitability of her escort. Grandfather was eager to marry her off—in a politically advantageous match, of course.

Phoebe paused in the palatial foyer. She could easily picture a bride sweeping down the wide marble staircase. An attractive blond hostess interrupted the mental image by greeting Carter by his first name then escorting them to a table in a private corner of what probably had been the formal drawing room of the private residence. Phoebe felt a spark of something that was certainly not jealousy each time the woman flashed Carter a blinding smile.

Candlelight flickered on the widely spaced tables and from wall sconces, giving the room an intimate air. Silverware and crystal glittered like diamonds in the soft light. Carter pulled out her chair and Phoebe noticed the single long-stemmed red rose on the snowy tablecloth in front of her chair. She sat and lifted the bud to inhale the heady fragrance. If this had been a true date she would have been bowled over by the romantic setting. But this wasn't a date, and she wasn't going to let herself be impressed. Much, she added grudgingly.

Carter seemed completely at ease with the opulent surroundings and deferential treatment. Twelve years ago he wouldn't have been. If the hostess's greeting hadn't clued Phoebe in to the fact that Carter had been here before then his ordering without consulting the menu would have. Her menu didn't list prices, but she didn't need them to know this dinner would be a far cry from the economical meals and picnics of their past. They'd never shared expensive dinners because Carter couldn't afford them and he'd refused to let her pay. The wine steward arrived, consulted with Carter and then departed.

Was the entire point of this evening to show her that he was now comfortable in her world? If so, why did he think she'd care? As if he'd read her thoughts he reached across the table and trapped her hand beneath his. Warmth traveled up her arm.

"It's good to see you again, Phoebe." His husky baritone and intent gaze made her stomach muscles quiver, and when his thumb stroked the inside of her wrist, she forgot to breathe. "Why don't we go into the next room and dance until our meal is ready?"

The thought of being in Carter's arms again made her light-headed, then an idea hit her with an ice-cold shower of sobriety. Did he think she'd tumble easily into his bed because of their past relationship? Well, he'd better think again. She wasn't a wide-eyed innocent any longer. She'd been wined and dined by some of the slickest politicians and political wannabes in the nation's capital—many of whom thought the best way to influence her grandfather was through her bed. She'd made a mistake once and become engaged before figuring out that she wasn't the main attraction in the relationship. The experience had been enough to make her question the motives of every man who asked her out.

Anger bubbled in her blood. How could Carter believe her to be so easy, so gullible? She concealed her annoyance with a polite smile the way her grandmother had taught her and extracted her hand. "I don't care to dance, thank you. How long have you been back in Chapel Hill?"

To give him credit, her failure to melt in her chair didn't throw him. "Three years. What about you? Where do you live?"

"I divide my time between Raleigh and D.C."

The wine arrived and Carter went through the tasting ritual. "Why are you still working with your grandfather?" he asked as soon as the steward departed.

Phoebe shifted in her seat and reached for her glass. "He needs me."

"And if his presidential bid fails, what will you do?"

Good question. The year before her grandmother passed away she'd made Phoebe promise to look out for her grandfather if anything ever happened to her. Phoebe often wondered if Gran had had a premonition that undiagnosed ovarian cancer would take her life so swiftly. After the funeral, Phoebe had put her plans on hold to help her grandfather through his grief. The months she'd expected had lapsed into years until Phoebe had been delaying her own plans for so long that she'd finally quit making them.

Phoebe was in one of those holding patterns Carter had mentioned earlier. Not that she regretted the years at her grandfather's side. She'd learned a lot, met world leaders and become very good at her job, so good in fact that she could work almost anywhere she wanted…. But if her grandfather's presidential bid failed, Phoebe didn't want to work for another politician. The joy of finding the poetry in the speeches had long since faded, and the appeal of twisting words to rouse patriotism or to hide blunders and weaknesses was gone. What kept her going was the knowledge that the work she did as part of her grandfather's team made a difference.

What would she do with her life once her grandfather retired? The question rattled her, but it deserved thoughtful consideration when she wasn't seated across from such a distraction.

She sipped her wine to alleviate the dryness in her mouth caused by fear of the unknown. Once upon a time, exploring the unfamiliar with Carter had thrilled her. Had she changed so much in the passing years? Had she become too much of a coward to try something new? "We're anticipating a successful campaign. Should the outcome not go as projected then I'll explore my alternatives."

"Time has a way of getting away from you, Phoebe. If you don't make decisions, the choices will dwindle until there are none."

She wanted to ask what had made him so bitter, but refrained because she didn't want to become involved. *Get the pictures. Get out.* "You're suggesting I live for the moment? Just selfishly grab whatever I want with both hands and damn the consequences?"

The way her parents had.

He probably thought she'd grab him if he played his cards right. Although the thought tempted her, she wasn't young and foolish any longer, and she didn't do casual sex, especially not in Washington where who was sleeping with whom was the gossips' favorite topic.

His gaze held hers. "I'm saying, figure out what you want and plot a strategy to achieve it before it's too late, unless of course, you want your grandfather to keep calling the shots for you. What do *you* want, Phoebe?"

Knotting her fingers in her lap, she snuffed out the question before she could answer it. It didn't really matter what she wanted. Her course had been set years ago. She would continue to write her grandfather's speeches and act as his hostess as she had since graduation from Georgetown University. If she didn't feel any enthusiasm for the plan, then the pictures were to blame. Once she no longer had to worry about them turning up in the press to humiliate her and anger her grandfather, she could get excited about the possibility of a whistle-stop tour of the country and later, living in the White House. In the meantime, she had research to do before she could begin drafting her grandfather's declaration of candidacy speech.

She pasted on her best campaign smile. "I want my grandfather to win the election. He is by far the best candidate. Let me tell you why."

Sortie one. A draw.

Carter folded his napkin at the end of the meal and battled frustration. Strategic withdrawal. Reevaluate the strategy. Approach from a different flank.

Phoebe had installed razor wire around herself in the past twelve years. She'd carefully sidestepped all personal questions and remained immune to every suggestive comment or look. Seducing her wouldn't be as easy as he'd expected.

A heavy hand descended on his shoulder. Carter jerked his gaze upward and found Sam at his shoulder. He rose and returned Sam's salute. "Great chow as usual, Sam."

"You're too kind, Captain," Sam said in a voice heavily laced with sarcasm. "Who's the pretty lady?"

Phoebe's eyes widened as she took in all six feet, six inches of his forty-year-old, hard-as-nails, kick-your-ass-and-enjoy-it friend. Sam would be one scary dude to run into in an alley, and he didn't look like any chef Carter had ever encountered, but he'd been a damned good Marine and a real team player.

"Phoebe, this is Sam Kalas. He kept our platoon fed. His cooking has been known to make a four-star general get on his knees and beg for seconds. Sam's the owner and chef of this place."

"Part owner," Sam corrected. "Without your bucks to back up my cooking, I'd still be slinging military rations and living in the barracks. Instead I get to cook food that looks and tastes good and live upstairs in these swanky digs."

Phoebe shot a surprised glance in Carter's direction and extended her hand to Sam. "My compliments to the chef."

"Thanks, ma'am." Sam's black eyes pinned Carter. "When Suzie told me you'd called for a reservation for two, I decided to come out to see who'd make you break your fast."

Carter's ears burned under Phoebe's speculative gaze. So he didn't date much these days. Big deal. CyberSniper came first. But Sam had handed him the perfect opportunity to pay Phoebe back for making their past dates a dirty secret. He let his mouth tip in a smile his corps buddy wouldn't misunderstand. "Phoebe's an old friend."

Sam's speculative gaze fixed on Phoebe's red cheeks. He nodded. "Nice meeting you, ma'am. I've been working on a new dessert recipe all week. Can I tempt you folks?"

"We really have to run," Phoebe replied before Carter could. "But thank you."

Carter considered the potency of Sam's concoctions and weighed the odds of salvaging the evening. Curiosity urged him to try any means at his disposal to see if Phoebe's kiss still packed the old punch he remembered. "How about a carry-out?"

A smartass grin spread across Sam's face. "Whatever you want, Captain."

With another sharp salute, Sam returned to the kitchen.

Phoebe's jaw and spine looked rigid enough to snap. "I won't have dessert with you."

The kiss Carter wanted looked like a slim possibility, but he'd always enjoyed fighting against the odds. "What makes you think I'm willing to share? But you don't know what you're missing, Phoebe. Sam's desserts are like sex in a spoon." He winked. "A smart woman would reconsider."

Three

"Try a little sin, Phoebe. You'll like it."

Phoebe shifted on her feet in the moonlight-flooded driveway of Carter's home and tried to ignore her body's traitorous response to the invitation in his huskily murmured words. Every self-preservation instinct within her screamed, *Run*, but she couldn't. Carter had her caged between his broad chest, the open door of his car and the seat she'd just vacated. A balmy evening breeze caressed her sensitized skin.

He passed the open container holding the rich-smelling chocolate dessert beneath her nose and her mouth watered.

"What do you know? Sam included a couple of disposable spoons." Carter scooped up a bite of the creamy concoction and lifted it to Phoebe's lips.

She shouldn't be tempted by the man or his decadent dessert. She'd never forgive herself for succumbing to the first, and her hips would pay the price for sampling the second. But this entire escapade with Carter was ill-advised and thorny, and she deserved a reward for holding strong against his potent charm all evening. It hadn't been easy.

She opened her mouth and Carter fed her. Dark chocolate, sweet cherry and rich cream flavors merged on her tongue. She closed her eyes in ecstasy. Heaven. Bliss. No, better. Rolling the tastes around in her mouth, she searched for the perfect words to describe the dessert without success.

She licked her lips. "That is truly amazing."

Carter set the container on the roof of his car and leaned closer until only inches separated their faces. His breath fanned her cheek and the look of intent in his eyes made her insides quiver.

"Almost as good as sex," he said a whisper away from her mouth. "Want to come in and share?"

Phoebe cursed her weakening knees and the way the fine hairs on her body rose to attention. My God, he was playing her and her stupid hormones were falling for it. She ignored the rapid pounding of her heart, blocked his forward progress with a hand to his chest and glared at him.

"Would you quit the Casanova routine already?"

He observed her through narrowed eyes. "You think I'm trying to put the moves on you?"

She arched an eyebrow and aimed for sarcasm, but it wasn't easy when her body ached for what he offered. "Aren't you? The question is why?"

His jaw shifted, then he rocked back on his heels and shoved his hands into his pants pockets, giving her some much-needed space. "I'm curious. Aren't you?"

"About what?" she asked even though she suspected she knew the answer.

"Whether it would be as good between us as it used to be."

Her stomach plunged to her pumps. Yes, the thought had

crossed her mind a few times since making the decision to seek out Carter, but she had no intention of satisfying her curiosity. The last time she had, he'd stolen her heart and shattered it into tiny irreparable fragments.

She forced a casual shrug and lied through a dismissive smile. "Not really. Now, if you don't mind, I need to get home. Enjoy your dessert."

Shoving past him, Phoebe beat a hasty retreat to her car. She fumbled with her seat belt until it clicked and glanced at Carter one last time before throwing the car in reverse. And then she remembered she'd forgotten to collect. Argh. She shoved the gearshift back into park, rolled down her window and stuck out her hand.

"The picture," she called, and wiggled her fingers. "Please get the picture. I'll wait here."

Carter sauntered toward her. His casual stride contradicted the stiff set of his shoulders and the determined line of his jaw made her skin prickle in alarm. She shifted uneasily in her seat. Carter reached into his breast pocket and withdrew a photo. A voice in Phoebe's mind shrieked in panic. He'd had one of their pictures in his pocket all evening. What if it had fallen out? What if—

And then Carter leaned down and folded his arms on her open window, choking off her thoughts with his nearness. "You really shouldn't rush off."

"I'm expecting a call," she said through teeth clamped together in an I'll-be-polite-even-if-it-kills-me smile.

He ignored her open hand and ducked through the window. Phoebe leaned back against the seat to give him as much room as possible as he reached across her body to tuck the picture into the outside pocket of the purse she'd set on the seat beside her. His scent surrounded her. Instead of depositing the photo and withdrawing from the car as she'd expected, he cupped her face in his warm hand. Before she could react, Carter's lips were on hers. Hot. Soft. Insistent.

Phoebe's breath lodged in her lungs. Heat steamed her skin. She wanted to push him away, but couldn't seem to instigate the action.

The magic is still there.

He sipped from her lips, lifting and nuzzling again. His thumb stroked over the pulse racing at the base of her throat and then traced her collarbone to the V of her neckline. Her nipples rose in anticipation of his touch. The slick heat of his tongue caressed her bottom lip, slipped past to tease her sensitive inner flesh and to skate over her clenched teeth. Overwhelming sensations poured down on her, stealing sanity and eroding her willpower. She was on the verge of giving in to the hunger and opening her mouth to taste him when he straightened and stepped away from the car.

"G'night, Phoebe. Call me when you think you can handle our second date." With a casual salute he headed back toward his house, grabbed the decadent dessert from the roof of his car and disappeared into the garage.

Phoebe released a frustrated breath. He'd gotten to her. Damn him. Well, it wouldn't happen again. She curled her trembling fingers around the steering wheel and backed out of the driveway.

Next time she'd be prepared for his devious moves.

With his pulse hammering in the triple digits, Carter stumbled into his house and collapsed in a kitchen chair. He'd feel smug about the success of his sneak attack if he weren't totally disgusted with himself.

He still wanted Phoebe with the panting lack of control of the boy he'd once been. The knowledge had hit him like a sniper's bullet the second his lips touched hers. He scrubbed a hand over the lower half of his face, but he couldn't erase the feel of her satiny lips or her sweet taste. He'd grossly underestimated his opponent's power.

He'd been about to write off the evening as an unsuccessful maneuver when she'd wriggled her fingers and sent a firestorm of memories streaking through his brain. She'd used the same gesture twelve years ago to invite him into her arms.

One thing was damned certain. He wouldn't be satisfied until he got Phoebe Lancaster Drew into his bed and out of his system. But she had his number and he didn't like it. She expected a seduction, so he'd have to scale back and be more subtle if he wanted to soften her up. A grin of anticipation tugged at his lips.

He retrieved a legal pad from the kitchen drawer and composed a list of ways to get Phoebe to let down her guard, then he reached for the phone. Date number two would require a little help from his friends.

"'Call me when you think you can handle our second date,'" Phoebe mimicked Carter's deep voice as she accelerated up his driveway and into the shade of an overhanging oak.

As if she could ignore a challenge like that. But still, she'd waited two days to call. Of course, that wasn't because she lacked nerve, but because the day after their first date had been the Memorial Day holiday. She groaned at the bald-faced lie…um…political whitewash.

Casual clothes. Tennis shoes. Nine o'clock tomorrow. Click. Her phone conversation with Carter gave new meaning to the term succinct. He hadn't allowed her the opportunity to argue or to ask him to reconsider ending this nonsensical game.

She shoved the gearshift into park, opened the car door and stepped into his driveway wearing her new cross-trainers.

Her heart rate doubled as she marched up the walk. The first date picture had been the one she'd already seen. Which one would Carter choose for today's mystery date? And would she shove it in the back of her nightstand drawer with the other one or would she destroy it?

Destroy it, she decided. She couldn't risk her grandfather finding it. The pictures were the only evidence of her wilder days. She didn't want him to fear that she was like her mother— an embarrassment and a liability to his political stature.

You're a selfish prima donna who never thinks of anyone but herself. Go. Go and don't come back until you've grown up.

If growing up means being a pretentious old windbag like you, then I'm never coming back.

Phoebe rubbed her temple, trying to erase the memories of that last explosive argument between her grandfather and mother. Despite the passage of twenty-three years, she could still hear the raised voices as clearly as she had that night from the top of the stairs.

Lesson learned. Never say things you can't take back.

Carter's front door opened, cutting off her unpleasant memories. One glance at his face flooded Phoebe with the memory of their misbegotten kiss. She shifted her gaze to the gray USMC T-shirt stretched across his broad chest. The barbed-wire tattoo winked from under the sleeve, mesmerizing her. She shook off her fascination and examined the rest of his attire. His cut-off shorts were only slightly less disreputable than the frayed ones he'd worn the last time. They revealed plenty of bare leg between the ragged hem and his running shoes.

Phoebe's neatly pressed linen shorts and sage knit polo top looked positively formal in comparison. "Where are we going?"

"Campus." He motioned for her to enter.

Being careful not to brush against him, she crossed the threshold and turned to face him in the foyer. His cologne eroded her hard-earned indifference. "The university campus? Why?"

"Bike ride."

She hadn't ridden a real bicycle since she'd been a student here in Chapel Hill, but all the clichés said it wasn't a skill you'd forget. And biking hardly seemed conducive to seduction. Had she misinterpreted his intentions or had Carter given up on the idea of getting her back into his bed?

Why did it bother her that he'd given up so easily?

"I don't own a bicycle."

"I borrowed one from my neighbor, and I bought you a helmet."

Excellent. Hat head. Not that she minded how she looked when she was with Carter. *So why did it take you an hour to choose your outfit this morning? And why did you buy new shoes last night?*

She followed him into the kitchen. "Fine. If it's a bike ride you want, I'm game. But where is the picture?"

"Impatient to see it?" His eyes gleamed with amusement.

Her skin prickled. She gnashed her back teeth. "I don't like the idea of it falling out of your pocket somewhere on campus."

"It won't."

"Leave it here."

He leaned back against the counter and crossed his ankles. "If you want to come in when we return, all you have to do is say so, Phoebe."

The smug smile dimpling his cheeks contradicted the ruthless glint in his sapphire eyes. She refused to inflate his ego with a response to his misinterpretation. "Carter, please leave the picture here."

He shrugged, pulled his wallet out of his back pocket and extracted the photo and laid it facedown on the counter.

She stepped forward and reached for it, but he slid it out of the way. "Uh, uh, uh. Patience. You have to earn your reward."

Reward, my foot. More like penance for allowing her selfish streak to rule her actions for those nine months. During that time she'd acted exactly like her mother and thought of no one but herself. Phoebe fisted her hands, fought her temper and glared at him. She hadn't realized how close they stood. Only inches separated their bodies and, with her head tilted back, all he had to do was lower his to kiss her. After that kiss the other night, she almost wanted him to. The thought shocked her into taking a giant step backward.

"Let's get this over with." How ungracious. Her grandmother would be appalled to know how miserably her etiquette instructions had failed.

Carter swept a hand toward the garage door. Phoebe led the way. She quickly noted two things. He'd hung the bikes on a rack on the back of the Mustang and lowered the car's convertible top. She might be happy to have the helmet after all—to cover her windblown hair. *Neatness counts*, her grandmother's voice echoed.

Resigned to her fate, Phoebe climbed into his car. The roar of the wind sweeping past the open top as they zipped down the road made conversation difficult—not a circumstance she minded. Within minutes they'd pulled into a parking space on one of the main streets through campus. Carter fed coins into the meter and then unloaded the bikes. One looked fast and lethal. The other looked more sedate. Phoebe hoped her loaner was the sedate one.

She tried to smooth her hair into the French twist on the back of her head, but feared she'd failed by the number of wisps teasing her cheeks and nape. Carter handed her a white helmet. She set it on her head, but it tilted awkwardly due to her upswept hair.

"Lose the bun."

"It's not a bun."

"Whatever. It interferes with the fit of the helmet and, therefore, your safety. Lose it," he repeated.

Phoebe hesitated.

"C'mon, Phoebe, let your hair down. It's only a bike ride, for crissake."

Why did she think his comment referred to loosening more than her hair? She removed the pins. Carter held out his hand and she dropped them into his palm. He carried them to the car while she struggled to finger-comb her hair. It fell in a tangled mess over her shoulders. She wished she had a mirror and then changed her mind. Better not to see how bad she looked. She plopped the helmet on her head and fumbled with the buckle.

"Let me help." Carter moved closer—too close—and adjusted the strap under her chin. Heat radiated off his body. The light touch of his warm fingers beneath her ears and on the skin of her jaw made her shiver. Embarrassed that he could get to her so easily, she closed her eyes and fought to regulate her breathing until he finished.

What seemed an eon later, he stepped back. Was that satisfaction glinting in his eyes? Maybe this bike ride wasn't as innocent as she'd thought. "A perfect fit."

"Where are we going?"

"I thought you might like to visit a few of your old haunts. Crowded sidewalks won't be a problem since only the summer school kids are here." He climbed on his bike—the one that looked as if it had been built for the Tour de France.

She awkwardly straddled the other. The fewer folks who witnessed her humiliation, the better. With any luck they wouldn't run into any camera-toting reporters. For the most part, the press ignored her—a circumstance she deliberately cultivated by living as boring a life as possible. They focused their cameras on her charismatic grandfather. Unfortunately the upcoming election campaign made her a person of interest, boring or not. "Lead on."

It didn't take Phoebe long to realize that riding a real bicycle up inclines and over bumpy terrain was nothing like riding a stationary exercise bike in the air-conditioned gym of the D.C. town house basement, but she quickly became accustomed to balancing the machine. That wasn't a good thing. Once she didn't have to worry about falling over, her mind and her gaze wandered to the buildings where she'd once attended classes, to the adorable chipmunks scampering across the ground…to the tight curve of Carter's backside and the wide expanse of his shoulders as he bent over his handle bars.

She ground her teeth at the number of coeds examining him with appreciative gazes and then shook her head. They could have him. One at a time. All at once. She didn't care.

"Ready for lunch?" Carter called over his shoulder.

"Sure." And then maybe she could finish this pointless ride down memory lane, return to his home, collect the picture and leave. Her pulse picked up speed in anticipation.

He coasted to a stop in front of the Student Union, climbed from his bike and walked it to the metal rack. Phoebe did the same. Her legs quivered. Apparently she wasn't in as good a shape as she'd thought. How long had they been riding, anyway? In her nervousness over today's outing she'd forgotten her watch—an error a punctual person like her never committed.

Carter secured both bikes with a cable lock and nodded toward a vacant table in the shade under the shelter. "Have a seat. I'll go inside and get lunch."

Phoebe wobbled toward the table and collapsed. She wouldn't give Carter the leverage of knowing that she'd been enjoying the ride through campus too much to notice her overtaxed muscles or what she suspected were blisters forming on her heels. No doubt she'd pay for her distraction, and her pride, tomorrow.

A young blonde ogled Carter's retreating backside. Phoebe caught herself glaring, averted her gaze and focused on the pit—a sunken brick courtyard where students gathered to mingle, protest or party. She felt positively ancient compared to the girl she'd been when she dined here years ago. Back then she'd been overflowing with hope, excitement and enthusiasm for a limitless future. She'd had so many choices…and now she had so few. Pressure mounted her shoulders.

Her grandfather wanted her to run for office when he retired. She didn't have even a smidgeon of desire to do so. He'd be hurt and angry when she told him she wanted to break the century-old family political tradition. She tried to comfort herself with the knowledge that she had a minimum of two and possibly even as many as ten years to find the courage to tell him.

In the meantime, she had to get through the dates with Carter without repeating any of her past mistakes.

What a difference a decade made.

Carter watched Phoebe through the Union window as he stood in line to order their lunch. She'd removed her bike helmet and set it on the table, revealing sexy, tumbled hair that reminded him too damned much of how she'd looked after they made love. Sunlight glinted off the dark, wavy strands that hung to the base of her shoulder blades. But that's where the similarities ended.

Phoebe's pressed, tailored shorts skimmed her slim hips and covered most of her long legs—a far cry from the old cut-off jeans she'd swiped from him. A pale green polo shirt gently draped her breasts—breasts that he thought were a tad larger than he remembered. Breasts he had every intention of exploring up close and personally.

He picked up the lunch tray and headed outside. The sadness on Phoebe's face put a hitch in his step. She'd loved being a student here, or so he'd thought. He'd expected her to enjoy today's outing and to recall the number of times they'd left the pit and raced back to his dorm room to immerse themselves in each other.

His fingers itched for the digital camera he always carried in his pocket. He'd taken other pictures today and she hadn't liked it, but right now she was unaware of his presence and fiddling with her blindingly white tennis shoe and the sissy little puff ball on the back of her below-the-ankle sock. He balanced the tray in one hand and snapped a shot with the other and then tucked the camera away and resumed his journey.

"Everything okay?" he asked as he set the tray on the table.

She jerked upright and neutralized her expression. "Fine."

He didn't believe her, but he passed her a tall paper cup of sweetened iced tea without arguing. "Lady's choice. I have two chili dogs, a double cheeseburger and a grilled chicken sandwich."

"And enough French fries to clog every artery from here to D.C." Her teasing smile—genuine, not one of those insincere political ones—caught him off guard. For a second she'd looked like the girl he used to know.

She eyed the chili dogs in the same hungry way Carter eyed his neighbor's freshly baked chocolate-chip cookies, but Phoebe reached for the chicken sandwich instead. Halfway through the meal she reached for a French fry. A look of guilty pleasure covered her face as she chewed. Flames sparked to life behind Carter's zipper. He'd seen that expression before—right before she'd taken him inside her wet heat.

He gulped his drink and reached for his burger. Operation Seduction was doomed to fail if he couldn't maintain detachment. She'd have him begging instead of the other way around, and that wouldn't do. He'd begged for her time before. Never again.

She snitched another fry.

"You don't have junk food in D.C.?"

"No. Granddad is on a restricted diet." She didn't speak again until she'd finished her meal. "Tell me about Sam."

Carter set down his cup and wiped his mouth with a paper napkin. He'd consumed his meal, but he hadn't tasted a thing. When had watching a woman eat become fascinating? "What do you want to know?"

"How did you two end up in business together? I mean, it seems a little odd—a computer specialist and a cook."

"He hauled my ass to safety when I busted my knee. I owe him."

"So you're financing his restaurant?"

"Least I could do. Besides, the property is a good investment. He's smart and has strong ideas for growing the business."

She studied him for a minute. What was going on behind those hazel eyes? And then she rose. Regret settled over her features. "You're a nice guy, Carter. You always were. Can we go now?"

For crying out loud, he'd had better compliments. Why did this one fill his chest with warmth? And why did it make the back of his neck prickle with guilt over his planned seduction? Besides, if he was such a nice guy, why had she said goodbye?

Irrelevant, Jones. Forget it. "Sure."

He cleaned up the remains of the meal and unlocked the bikes. He and Phoebe pedaled toward the car through the vine-covered arboretum. They'd stolen more than kisses under the leafy canopy on cool autumn nights when his dorm room and hers were occupied. The memories made his bike seat uncomfortable. Good thing a cure for this obsession was around the corner. And no, dammit, that wasn't guilt squeezing his lungs. Phoebe would be just as willing as he by the time they hit the sheets.

She laughed at a pair of scampering chipmunks and Carter nearly plowed into a concrete bench. Her smile twisted something inside him and he silently swore. This date wasn't going as planned. Instead of softening Phoebe, he seemed to be the one going soft—except in one crucial area.

Phoebe's heart pounded and her palms dampened. Which picture would it be?

She followed Carter into the house, trying very hard not to wince as her shoes rubbed against her heels and her legs protested the unaccustomed exercise. She needed a long soak in a hot bath in the worst kind of way, and she prayed her muscles wouldn't lock up during the thirty-five-minute drive back to her grandfather's house.

"Drink?"

Phoebe jerked her gaze from the facedown photo on the counter to Carter. "No thanks, I should go."

He lifted the rectangle and studied it. Heat flared in his eyes and her own pulse flickered in response. Phoebe extended her hand. Carter offered the picture, but held it just out of her reach. Phoebe lunged forward and her right heel stung like a bee sting. Her breath hissed through her teeth.

"What's wrong?" His eyebrows and then the hand holding the picture lowered.

Her blister must have popped. She shifted her weight to her left foot. "Nothing. Could I have the picture, please?"

"Phoebe?" His gaze traveled down her body in a slow sweep. "You're bleeding."

"What?" She glanced down and saw the small red stain spreading on the back of her white bootie.

"Sit."

She startled at the barked command. "Excuse me?"

"Sit down and take off your shoes." The rigid line of his jaw and shoulders made him look very much like a man used to giving orders. She could get her fill of orders back home. Her grandfather's reputation for being the most inflexible member of the senate had been earned honestly.

"Carter, I'm capable of rendering my own first aid. Just give me the picture and let me go home."

In the blink of an eye he'd slung the snapshot onto the counter, swept her into his arms and set her down on the cool granite surface beside the microwave. He tackled her shoelaces despite her protests and swatting hands, removed her shoes and socks, then carefully lifted and examined her heels—first one and then the other. When he met her gaze, Phoebe sucked in a sharp breath at the anger blazing in his eyes.

"Why in the hell didn't you speak up?" His quiet voice could not conceal his fury.

"Because I didn't think it was as bad as this." And she hadn't. Sure, she'd realized before lunch that her new shoes were uncomfortable, but she hadn't expected blisters this size or blood. She would have said something. She wasn't a masochist.

"Don't move." He jabbed a finger in her direction, turned and strode from the room. Phoebe considered ignoring his dictate, snatching up the picture and racing out the door in her bare feet. She eyed the facedown square on the counter. Her pulse thudded erratically as she lifted the photo and turned it over. Memories washed over her as she examined the image from her past and her lungs jammed.

In this black-and-white photo Phoebe had draped herself

across Carter's lap in his desk chair. Her arm, loosely wrapped around his neck, blocked her breasts from the camera, and her bottom covered his groin, but there was no denying they were both naked and having a very good time. She remembered squirming in a deliberate attempt to arouse him. His dimpled grin promised retribution. As with the previous picture, nothing had been going on when the camera's shutter clicked, but immediately afterward she'd turned, straddled his lap, taken him inside and loved him until he'd begged for mercy.

Her skin flushed and moisture flooded her mouth. She hadn't found passion like that since—not that she'd done much looking since she tried to avoid the gossips' tongues. Closing her eyes, Phoebe struggled for composure and tried to recall the pain that had followed her breakup with Carter, but it wasn't as easy to recollect as before. When she lifted her lids she discovered Carter leaning against the doorjamb watching her. The rigidity of his jaw and his muscles contradicted his casual pose.

His gaze burned into hers and then dropped to her mouth. Her lips felt incredibly dry and the urge to wet them nearly overwhelmed her, but she resisted, fearing he might see the gesture as an invitation for another one of his mind-melting kisses. She shoved the picture into her pocket, gripped the edge of the cool countertop and took an unsteady breath.

Carter yanked a kitchen chair toward her, sat and opened the first-aid box in his lap. "This is going to sting."

She barely had a moment to ponder his roughened voice before fire consumed her heel and licked up her leg. Phoebe gritted her teeth and blinked back tears as Carter quickly and efficiently disinfected each blister, smoothed on antibacterial ointment and applied bandages.

He stood and shoved the chair under the table with anger evident in every short, jerky movement. He returned to cup each of her knees with big, hot hands. "Of all the damned fool things to do. What were you thinking? Scratch that. You weren't thinking."

His hot gaze fastened on her lips. Her heart stalled and then resumed beating at a sprinter's pace. Carter was going to kiss her. Worse, she had a sneaking suspicion she wanted him to—even though it would be a colossal mistake. She cleared her throat. "I need to go."

He didn't move. For several tense seconds Carter held her gaze. Anger drained from him in noticeable increments, loosening the hard edge of his jaw, relaxing the unyielding set of his shoulders, and finally, softening the grip of his hands on her legs. Arousal sparked in his eyes and Phoebe's common sense screamed, *Leave while you can.* But she didn't move.

His palms skated upward from her knees at a snail's pace. The tips of his fingers slipped beneath the hem of her shorts and teased the sensitive skin at the tops of her thighs. Her breath hitched and goose bumps chased over her skin. He moved forward, nudging his way between her legs and trapping her on the counter with the powerful one-two punch of his body and a paralyzing hormone rush.

Phoebe wet her lips, tilted her head back and lost herself in the blue flames of passion burning in his eyes. His gaze returned to her lips and, impossibly, grew hotter. Need twisted low in her abdomen. She swallowed and inhaled shakily.

"Carter, we shouldn't." The firm warning she'd intended came out as a jagged, wanton whisper.

"Phoebe." His husky murmur made her shiver.

His breath swept her mouth a split second before his lips seared hers. Carter tasted her, probing, exploring and savoring her mouth one silky stroke at a time. Then he angled his head and started over again. The force and hunger of his second kiss pressed her head against the overhead cabinets.

Phoebe's equilibrium shifted. *Push. Him. Away.* She lifted her hands and dug her fingers into his waist, but instead of shoving, she held on for dear life as her world went topsy-turvy. The chemistry between them always had been strong, but nothing like this instantaneous, all-consuming rush of desire that made her impatient and greedy for things she couldn't have.

Carter transferred his grip to her buttocks, cupping her and pulling her to the edge of the counter until his hard flesh pressed against her center. Phoebe moaned into his mouth. The needy sound jarred her. A fragment of reason urged her to end this before it went too far. She lifted her hands to his chest and her palms curved over his pectorals, derailing her good intentions. In a weak last-ditch effort to break his hypnotic hold, she tried and failed to circle the supple skin of his biceps with her fingers. Suddenly learning his new shape, testing the firmer, harder texture of his muscles seemed of utmost importance. Her hands found the breadth of his back, exploring the additional depth and power of him.

Carter shuddered in her arms. His hot hands found her breasts. He cradled her and rubbed circles over her distended nipples with his thumbs. The hunger in her belly intensified. She leaned into him, pressing against the heat and hardness of his chest. Carter groaned her name, tangled his fingers in her hair and tugged until her head tilted to the side, baring her throat for a thorough exploration. He traced her ear with his tongue, laved her pulse point and nipped her tender skin.

Phoebe wanted more. She wanted to feel his supple skin against hers. She lifted her feet to wrap her ankles around his tight butt. Pain shot up her legs. Gasping, she jerked free and whacked her head on the cabinet behind her. "Ow."

Carter jerked back. "What?"

"My heels." The heat of passion turned into the burn of shame. She'd clung to him like a spiderweb despite her vow not to do so. Phoebe shoved Carter out of the way and hopped down from the counter. Ignoring the tenderness of her heels, the unsteadiness of her overworked thighs and now her aching head, she snatched up her shoes. "I have to go."

And she ran.

Four

No more romanticized recollections of the past.

No more wondering what might have been.

And *definitely* no more kisses.

Phoebe Lancaster Drew, you are a weak opponent, and weakness leads to defeat. Or so her grandfather said.

Priority number one. Fortify her resistance. Done.

Phoebe squared her shoulders, steered her sedan into Carter's driveway and parked beneath the oak tree. For four days she'd jumped each time the phone rang, but Carter hadn't called, and when she'd tried to phone him at home, his machine had picked up. She hadn't left a message for fear he'd hear the desperation in her voice. She'd debated forgetting about the pictures and walking away from their bargain, but with so much to lose that wasn't a valid option.

While researching her grandfather's competition, she'd given in to the urge to research Carter. Her Internet search had turned up not only the name of his company, CyberSniper, but also a surprising number of magazine articles about Carter's impressive business acumen, his company's rapid growth and even his biography.

She shouldn't have wasted time reading the articles, but she hadn't been able to stop herself. She'd learned that Carter had spent eight years in the Marine Corps in the field of electronic surveillance and specialized communications. When a skirmish between rival factions had broken out in a small village he'd raced through enemy fire to save a five-year-old girl rather than take cover. In the process he'd received a gunshot wound that had shattered his kneecap and ended his military career.

She'd also read about his company and quickly discovered that Carter Jones had become a force to be reckoned with in the field of creating secure networks and tracking computer crimes. Phoebe had been proud of him even though she had no right to be.

By the fifth day of waiting for Carter to call, she'd been so tense she couldn't eat or sleep. She'd decided to be proactive and dialed his office first thing Monday morning only to learn that Carter had been called out of town the day after their last encounter, but he was expected to return this afternoon.

So once again, going against every etiquette lesson her grandmother had taught her, Phoebe arrived at Carter's home uninvited. Her strategy: to confront him and renegotiate their deal, or at the very least, to speed things along. She couldn't be sneaking out to meet Carter once her grandfather returned home in three weeks.

She exited her car. Ten steps later she slowed her power-walk pace. Why race up his front walk as if she couldn't wait to see him again? That certainly wasn't the case. She rounded the fragrant gardenia bushes and jerked to a halt at the sight of a jeans-clad bottom—a *female* jeans-clad bottom—bent over the flower pots on Carter's front porch. The woman straightened and turned. Phoebe caught herself gaping at an attractive, dark-haired, barefoot and very *pregnant* woman.

There were no other vehicles in the driveway and bare feet ruled out an employee, didn't they? Phoebe's heart stalled and her teeth closed with an audible click. So Carter did have someone special in his life. And she was expecting a baby. Carter's baby? Phoebe's chest burned, reminding her to inhale.

"Hello," the woman offered with a questioning smile.

Calling upon every ounce of self-discipline she owned, Phoebe gathered herself. "Good evening. Is Carter in?"

"He'd better be since it's his turn to cook dinner. I'm Lily, and you are…?" The woman pulled off her leather work gloves and extended her hand.

"Phoebe…an acquaintance of Carter's." Phoebe swallowed and shook hands politely, but her insides twisted like a waterspout. Her reaction was ridiculous. She wasn't in love with Carter anymore. She didn't even like this newer, harder version of him or the games he insisted on playing—even if she did find him physically attractive—so why did her skin suddenly feel too tight?

"Nice to meet you, Phoebe." The woman thrust open Carter's front door without knocking and called as she entered, "Carter, you have company."

An employee definitely wouldn't barge in without knocking. With her heart pounding, Phoebe followed Lily inside. Carter, once again wearing disreputable cut-off jeans and a T-shirt, strolled out of the hall leading to the kitchen. He carried a long-necked beer bottle in one hand. Though he looked relaxed, there were dark shadows beneath his eyes and beard stubble covered the lower half of his face. As soon as he spotted her, he halted and his expression hardened. "Phoebe."

Phoebe swallowed to ease the dryness in her mouth. "I didn't mean to interrupt."

Carter's woman touched Phoebe's elbow. "You're not interrupting. Join us for dinner. Trust me, there's plenty of food. Isn't there, Carter?"

Carter's gaze jerked to the statuesque beauty's and then returned to Phoebe's. "I'm sure Phoebe has other plans."

That Carter didn't want her here couldn't be clearer. His hard stare ordered her to confirm his statement, but the strangest thing happened. Phoebe's righteous streak—the one that hated political whitewashing and backslapping—reared its ugly head. She didn't want to hurt Lily. The woman seemed genuinely nice, and was perfectly innocent in Carter's scheme, but Phoebe wanted to make Carter as uncomfortable as he'd made her recently. If Lily was carrying his child, then Carter needed to understand exactly what he could lose by pursuing these dates.

She forced a smile. "Actually, my evening is completely free. I'd love to stay for dinner, Lily. Thank you for your gracious invitation."

Carter's eyes narrowed in warning.

Lily grinned. "Great. I'll set another place at the table."

She disappeared through the archway, leaving Carter and Phoebe alone in the foyer.

"We didn't have a date," he said in a low, rumbly voice as if he didn't want Lily to overhear.

"We have unfinished business, and you didn't call. If you'd like to hand over the negatives and the rest of the pictures right now, I'll suddenly recall a prior engagement."

"I didn't call because I've been out of town and both your cell phone and your grandfather's home numbers are unlisted. No deal on the pictures."

Right. She'd called him last time and she'd been so flustered by his kiss that she hadn't given him her number after their second date.

Phoebe looked beyond his shoulder and met his gaze again. "Are you sure you want to risk Lily finding out about our past and our current bargain."

Surprise flashed in his eyes and one corner of his mouth twitched. "The facts won't change her feelings for me."

Carter had changed over the years, but Phoebe hadn't expected him to become an overconfident jerk. Didn't he care that Lily could be hurt by their arrangement? Did he believe a woman would be so bowled over by his handsome face, beefcake body and sexy tattoo that she'd forgive him for cheating?

"You're making a mistake, Carter."

He casually sipped his beer and let his gaze glide over her. "I'll risk it. How are your heels?"

Her skin, already warm in the wake of his visual caress, burned at the reminder of their last encounter. She'd been shameless. "Fine."

"Good." He swept an arm toward the kitchen. "Come in. If you insist."

Phoebe preceded him down the short hall, but stopped on the threshold of the kitchen in surprise. Two men and another woman were gathered around the table, looking through a stack of eight-by-ten photos. A dark-haired toddler, whom Phoebe recognized as the one in the picture hanging on Carter's refrigerator, played with an assortment of toys on the floor.

The warmth of Carter's palm on her back startled her. He urged her forward. "Phoebe, you remember Sawyer and Rick, don't you? This is Lynn, Sawyer's wife, and J.C., my godson. You met Rick's wife Lily outside. Lily also happens to be my landscaper. She can't keep her hands out of my pots."

Phoebe ignored his teasing remark as reality hit her square

in the face. Lily was his neighbor, not his lover. Carter had known exactly what she'd thought and hadn't corrected her. The rat. She glared at him and then shifted her gaze to the others. Phoebe's muscles tensed when she met the men's hostile expressions. She hadn't recognized Rick or Sawyer, but upon closer inspection, their features looked familiar. They'd matured well, though not with Carter's amazing improvements, and they obviously remembered Phoebe's and Carter's past relationship—not fondly, judging by the scowls directed her way.

What had Carter told them about the breakup, and had he shown them the pictures? He'd dodged her question when she'd asked who else had seen them, and this trio had been extremely close. *Had Sawyer and Rick seen her naked?* Embarrassment raced through Phoebe like a grass fire. She wanted to leave, but she wouldn't give Carter the satisfaction of seeing her run.

Lynn rose from the table, smiling. "It's nice to meet you, Phoebe. Come in. We're admiring Carter's most recent batch of photographs."

Phoebe wiped her damp palms on her slacks and faced Carter. During college he'd worked a deal with one of his physics professors granting him unlimited use of the department's darkroom. "Do you still have access to a darkroom?"

"I have a fully equipped one in my basement that puts the old university one to shame, but digital photography and scanners have made darkrooms virtually unnecessary. Want a beer?"

He could print more of their damning photos anytime he pleased. Panic clawed her chest and her nails bit into her palms. "No. Thank you."

"What brings you back to Chapel Hill, Phoebe?" Sawyer asked in a cool, ultrapolite voice.

"I, uh…" She didn't dare tell the truth.

"Phoebe's feeling nostalgic," Carter answered for her.

Phoebe's nerves stretched tighter as she waited for him to elaborate, but he didn't.

"I hope you're not," Sawyer said with a stern stare at Carter.

Carter shrugged. His gaze traveled over Phoebe as potent as a lingering caress. Her pulse rioted. "Some parts of the past are worth repeating."

"And some aren't," Rick added.

The women's gazes ping-ponged between the men. Frowns pleated their eyebrows and curiosity filled their expressions. Obviously they sensed there was more to the story. Phoebe had no intention of filling them in.

Lily set the dishes on the table and turned to Phoebe. "You knew these guys in college?"

Phoebe didn't want to pursue this line of questioning, but didn't know how to avoid it. "Yes."

"How?"

"Carter was my computer science tutor." Phoebe glanced at Carter. His lips flattened and a muscle jumped in his jaw. He arched a challenging eyebrow, compelling Phoebe to add, "And we…dated."

The women exchanged a look Phoebe couldn't interpret and then Lily smiled. "Were these guys as tight back then as they are now?"

"They were very close." At least they had been until Carter's time with Phoebe had separated the trio. She'd lost count of the times Sawyer's unexpected return to the dorm room had caught them off guard and undressed.

Lynn pulled a photo of her husband and son from the stack and handed it to Carter. "Could you enlarge this one for me? I'd love to hang it behind my desk at the office."

Carter opened another round of beers for the men and poured a glass of iced tea. "How big do you want it? Poster-size like the last one?"

He handed the glass of tea to Phoebe. Their fingers and gazes touched. Her heart leaped to her throat when she imagined him printing poster-size versions of their private pictures, and she suspected from the glint in his eyes that he knew exactly what she was thinking, how much it terrified her, and he enjoyed her mental anguish.

"Carter's an excellent photographer," Lynn said.

"Yes." Phoebe could barely choke the word out past the constriction of her throat.

"Have you seen his photo albums? I love the pictures of these guys during their university days." Lynn's words created a snarl of dread in Phoebe's stomach.

"No, I haven't."

"I'll get them," Lynn said, and rose from the table.

"We don't want to bore Phoebe with the past." Carter stopped her with a hand on her shoulder.

"Go ahead, Lynn," Lily overrode Carter's objection. "Let's see if we can find any pictures of Phoebe."

Phoebe's stomach hit rock bottom as Lynn picked up her son and the women headed toward Carter's bedroom as if they had every right to do so. That the women could wander at will around his house said a lot about the closeness of their friendship. Carter lifted his beer bottle as if asking, *Happy now?* No, she wasn't happy. She'd wanted to make him squirm, but she was the one squirming.

Sawyer rose. "The grill should be ready."

Carter retrieved a platter of meat from the refrigerator and led his friends out the back door, leaving Phoebe alone in the kitchen. She exhaled a long, slow breath and sank into a chair at the table. What had she gotten herself into?

She glanced at the stack of pictures on the table. Unable to resist, she pulled them closer and caught her breath. Carter always had been a gifted photographer, but his skill had improved tenfold. If she hadn't read the articles about his successful company she'd suggest he make his living with his camera. She'd attended galleries with poorer quality exhibits. His understanding of light and composition made the black-and-white pictures look more like works of art than candid snapshots, and he'd done a remarkable job of capturing the emotion in his subjects' eyes.

He'd taken several pictures of her during their last date. It bothered her that he might have seen something in her eyes that she'd rather not reveal.

The women returned with a thick leather-bound photo album. Lynn set it in the center of the table and opened the cover. The image of the young man Phoebe had fallen in love with grinned back at her from a group shot of guys in the computer lab. She stared and pressed a hand over her thumping heart.

"Carter certainly has changed," Lynn remarked.

"Yes." Even as a lanky computer geek Carter's dimpled smile had the power to weaken Phoebe's knees and muddle her thoughts. He'd been kind and gentle and soft-spoken— so unlike her dogmatic grandfather. But Carter had changed. If he had any soft edges left, she hadn't seen them. More often than not the hard glint in his eyes made her uneasy.

Lily and Lynn chatted as they turned the pages and found pictures of their husbands, but Phoebe barely heard their words. She'd been sucked back into the past, into a time when she'd loved deeply and been immeasurably happy. Emotion welled up inside her. She struggled to conceal her reaction from the women beside her.

Phoebe didn't need to see the dates written below the photos in Carter's bold handwriting to know when she'd come into his life. The new confidence in his posture spoke of a man who'd discovered his sex appeal. There were pictures she remembered taking with his camera. Toward the end of the book she could tell when they'd broken up by the sadness in Carter's eyes.

She'd hurt him. For some reason, she'd always believed she was the only one who'd suffered from their breakup. He'd certainly walked away easily enough. She looked out the window to where he manned the grill, but he had his back to her.

On the last page of the album Carter stood between Sawyer and Rick. Tall and erect in his Marine uniform, he wore a grave expression on his face. His hair had been buzzed military-recruit short, which had only accentuated the angularity of his features.

"That's odd. You weren't in any of the pictures. How long did you say you and Carter dated?"

Lily's question made Phoebe's stomach churn. She'd tried so hard to erase Carter from her past. It hurt to know he'd already banished her memories. Or had he kept her pictures in a different location—perhaps with the intimate ones? No matter. Their past was over and they had no future.

"A few months. My grandmother died in December during my first semester. I transferred to a university out of state to be closer to…the rest of my family." She didn't want to give too many details since her purpose in seeking out Carter was confidential. If these women hadn't connected her with the senator, Phoebe would prefer to keep it that way.

Lynn smiled. "That's too bad, but now you're back. Carter needs a woman in his life, and I think it's sweet that you've come looking for him after all these years."

Surprise skittered up Phoebe's spine. "Oh, no, you don't understand. I'm not here to rekindle our roman—our relationship."

Lily's eyes narrowed. "Then why are you here?"

Trapped by her own confession, Phoebe forced a smile. "Just catching up. When is your baby due, Lily?"

"What does she want?" Sawyer asked. He nodded toward Phoebe on the other side of the French doors.

Carter sipped his beer and turned his back to the house, but the move didn't make him any less conscious of Phoebe in his kitchen. He'd swear her perfume clung to him because he could still smell her. "What makes you think she wants something?"

"Why else would she show up after all this time?"

He flipped the steaks and weighed his answer. He didn't kiss and tell. Nobody knew about the sexy pictures except him and Phoebe. He'd left Sawyer the key to his bank safe-deposit box with specific instructions. If Carter had been killed while in the service, Sawyer was to retrieve and destroy the envelope inside the box without breaking the seal. He'd trusted his buddy to do as asked.

"Her grandfather's getting ready to launch his presidential campaign. Phoebe wants to tie up a few loose ends." Dammit. He'd wanted to make their dates public, but he hadn't planned to drag her back into his circle of friends. That seemed too personal.

Yeah, like sleeping with her wouldn't be personal? No. Emotions wouldn't enter into his seduction plot. He'd execute his plan swiftly and expediently without putting his heart on the line. Sentiment was messy. He had a blown knee to prove it.

Rick snorted in disgust. "You're a loose end? Watch her, man. The last time she screwed you over you went off and joined the Marines. You're damned lucky you didn't get yourself killed because of her. Send her home and forget about her. You're too tired to think straight."

Wrong. Carter had worked around the clock for the past four days trying to repair a foolproof security system that some fool had managed to corrupt, but his exhaustion had vanished the moment he'd spotted Phoebe in his front hall. His pulse had yet to regain its regular rhythm—a fact he seriously resented.

"I didn't go off half-cocked. Sawyer and I had discussed enlisting together."

Sawyer straightened abruptly from where he leaned against the deck railing. "An idea that you scrapped the minute you met Phoebe." He snapped his fingers. "Wait a minute. Phoebe looked like she was about to pass out when our wives mentioned your photo albums. Do you have pictures of Phoebe? Pictures she wouldn't want to get out?"

An accurate—but lucky—guess considering Carter never went anywhere without a camera. He'd never lied to his buddies before and he didn't intend to start now, but some things a guy didn't share. "Look, she's back, and for some reason I still find her attractive. My plan is to spend some time with her and get her out of my system. Like the song says, 'This ain't no thinking thing.' It's just sex."

Rick started shaking his head before Carter finished speaking. "Never take a woman to bed with the intention of getting her out of your system. It doesn't work. Trust me, she'll only imbed herself deeper under your skin."

"That isn't going to happen. Phoebe showed me what she thought of me when she refused to meet my parents. I'm no wet-behind-the-ears boy who can be led around by my libido anymore."

Sawyer and Rick shared a look and laughed as if they knew something he didn't. Sawyer slapped Carter's back. "I hate to break it to you, man, but we can all be led around by our libidos. You're playing with fire, Carter. Let her go."

"I have my strategy mapped out. I know what I'm doing."

Rick gave him a pitying look. "You can't treat a woman or

a relationship like a war game. Cut your losses before this blows up in your face."

"I know what I'm doing," Carter repeated.

Sawyer shook his head. "Famous last words, pal. Don't say we didn't warn you."

Dinner had been absolute torture on many different levels.

Phoebe took a cleansing breath as Carter left the kitchen to escort the last of his guests out. Lily and Lynn had played matchmaker throughout the meal while their husbands had clearly wished Phoebe elsewhere. And Carter... At times Phoebe had caught glimpses of the man she remembered instead of the one bent on irritating her, and watching Carter play with his godson had made her yearn for what might have been despite her earlier vow not to do so. She smoothed back her hair and cursed the emptiness in her chest.

Abruptly rising from the table, she busied herself with tidying the kitchen and loading the dishwasher in an effort to stave off the unproductive thoughts, but the nagging questions forced themselves forward. If she and Carter had married after she graduated from the university, as they'd once planned, would they have had children by now? If so, how many? Could she have had this life and these tight-knit friends instead of an all-consuming career and a failed engagement and still kept her grandfather happy? No, Carter had asked her to choose between him and her grandfather, and she'd never, ever, turn her back on Granddad.

Ironically, because Carter's business successes and military background would make him a political asset, her grandfather would probably accept him as a suitor now, but Phoebe no longer wanted him. He'd hurt her too badly, and he'd released the selfish streak within her that she fought so hard to suppress—the same selfishness that had taken her parents from her. Her parents—especially her mother—had always dived into their causes with total abandon, disregarding the costs to their loved ones. During that nine months with Carter, Phoebe had been just as self-centered and thoughtless of others.

She shut the door on the dishwasher and on her thoughts and turned to see Carter leaning against the doorjamb. The predatory gleam in his eyes made her skin tingle.

"Enjoy yourself?" Sarcasm laced his voice.

"Yes, I did." As uncomfortable as the evening had been at times, she didn't regret it. Sitting at the table with the other couples had brought her to a very important conclusion. She wanted a relationship. No, she didn't intend to fall passionately in love ever again. The risks were too great. Instead, she wanted to find a man she could like and respect, one who would share her life and give her a family—one who wouldn't be using her to get to her grandfather.

She needed a safe and soft, muted watercolor relationship instead of a love affair as intense and passionate as an oil painting. A partner who dressed in business suits would fit into her world better than one who wore muscle-baring casual clothing. She definitely didn't want a man who could addle her thoughts and make her heart flutter by merely being in the same room. As soon as she returned to Washington, Phoebe intended to work less and date more in an effort to find this man. In fact, she'd accept the next invitation that came her way because she didn't want to be alone. Once her grandfather was gone, she'd have no one.

"What do you want, Phoebe?" Carter's terse question yanked her back to the present.

"You know what I want. The pictures. All of them. And the negatives."

"We have a deal."

"Carter, what purpose will it serve to prolong this?"

He shrugged one shoulder. "What will it hurt?"

She clenched her fists in frustration. "I don't have time for games, and now that I know you have the capability of reproducing our private photos in multiples or poster-size, why should I trust you?"

"I've always had that ability." He shoved off the jamb and closed the gap between them. Phoebe took a half step back, but the cool granite countertop of the kitchen island blocked her retreat. Carter stopped just inches away. Her pulse accelerated. "You once trusted me with everything."

His low-pitched words sent a ripple of arousal through her. Their love had known no boundaries. But the pain of his desertion had been equally bottomless. "I'm no longer a naive girl. My grandfather's campaign and my career are at stake."

"A career you're not crazy about."

She inhaled sharply at the accuracy of his statement. His cologne teased her nostrils and his chest touched hers. Her traitorous nipples puckered instantly. "I never said that."

"You didn't have to. You don't have plans or goals and the fire of excitement is gone from your eyes. Your heart's not in it."

She hadn't fooled him, but she'd fooled everyone else— including her grandfather. "Frankly, that's not your concern, and this bargain of yours reeks of extortion."

"It's only extortion when threats are involved. I'm not threatening you with anything except memories." He stroked a fingertip along her jawline and over her bottom lip. Desire coiled low in Phoebe's abdomen and alarm bells clanged in her subconscious.

"What are you afraid of, Phoebe?"

Of losing everyone and everything she held dear. "Nothing."

"Good. I don't want you afraid of me…or of this." He lowered his head and kissed her. Phoebe jerked in surprise, but

Carter's fingers cupped her nape, holding her captive while his embrace wreaked havoc on her equilibrium. His other hand settled at her waist, burning her through her clothing.

His lips teased, invited, seduced. The call of the wild drummed in her ears and her resistance melted like sugar in the rain. Oh, this was not good. She fought the urge to tangle her fingers in his short hair and shoved against the hard wall of his chest. "Give me the pictures, Carter."

He released her, but didn't move away. As close as they stood she could still feel the heat of his body calling to hers like a siren's song, but she wasn't about to bash herself against this rock again. He'd left her battered and bruised the last time, and because her grandfather hadn't known about Phoebe's relationship with Carter, she'd had to pretend everything was fine even though her world had been shattered.

Carter's jaw shifted and his eyes narrowed. "I'm leaving for Atlanta on Wednesday. I'll be gone for five days. Come with me. I'll give you all of the pictures and negatives when we return."

Audacious requests were nothing new. Politicians excelled at issuing them, but Carter's confounded her and his nearness clouded her ability to separate fact from filibuster. She put the width of the kitchen island between them and searched for a logical reason to his illogical request. "You're joking."

"I'll have to oversee my team for part of each day. While I'm working you'll have time to shop or work or whatever, but your evenings and nights will belong to me."

She blinked at the forthright statement and gaped at him. "You expect me to barter sex for the pictures?"

"They'll be yours whether or not we share a bed."

"And if I refuse?"

He shrugged. "Then I'll see you next week. We'll continue with our previous deal—one picture per date. I have a full calendar between now and the new year. If we can manage one date per week we're looking at a period of three to four months, possibly longer if I get called out of town again."

Her grandfather would be home in three weeks. Phoebe had to acquire all of the damning photos before then or she'd have to explain where she was going, with whom and why, and it wasn't unheard of for her grandfather to hire a private detective to run a background check on anyone she dated more than a couple of times. No telling what that would turn up. She suppressed a shudder.

Short of breaking in and stealing the photos, she had no choice. And wouldn't the arrest of a presidential candidate's granddaughter make lovely headlines? Carter's crazy request could work in her favor. Fewer people would recognize her in Atlanta than in North Carolina. "I insist on separate rooms."

"Done."

"I won't sleep with you."

"You've always had the right to say no, Phoebe." He braced his arms on the counter and leaned forward. The tattoo shifted as his bicep bunched, momentarily distracting her. She blinked to clear her head.

She'd never been very good at refusing Carter anything, but she wasn't an eighteen-year-old any longer. She'd become a woman with a backbone and an agenda, and she could avoid difficult issues. She did so every day on the job.

"Deal."

Five

The success of his plan, Carter decided, lay in its simplicity. Soften. Seduce. Sayonara.

"You promised separate rooms," Phoebe said from behind him as he opened the hotel room door.

"This is a two-bedroom suite." He'd avoided using a bellhop in anticipation of her reaction.

When she remained in the hall, he propped the door open with his suitcase and, carrying her luggage, preceded her into the sitting room. The bottle of Chateau Cheval Blanc he'd ordered waited in an ice bucket on the table in front of a wall of windows overlooking the Atlanta skyline. A glass-domed lid covered a tray of fruits, cheeses and finger foods that would tide them over until dinner. He'd come a long way from the tightly budgeted college kid she'd dated. Three-hundred-dollar bottles of wine and penthouse suites were now within his budget—not that he indulged in either often. He only dragged out the big guns when he had someone to impress—such as his father or Phoebe.

Carter Jones might not be old money like Phoebe's ancestors, but if the politician's disclosure records were accurate, then Carter could now meet the senator on a level playing field. His net worth exceeded Lancaster's—something that never would have happened on a military salary.

Carter inspected the bedrooms located on opposite sides of the sitting area and nodded his satisfaction in finding a king-size bed in each. He set Phoebe's suitcase on the luggage rack in the room containing the vase of roses he'd ordered. How long would it be before he joined her in that bed? Anticipation hummed in his veins. He considered the likelihood of failing in this mission slim to none. Phoebe would be breathless and satiated before they left Atlanta. But more important than that, he intended to be cured of his illogical fascination with her long before they checked out of the hotel.

Phoebe, clutching her laptop computer case like a lifeline, stood in the center of the sitting room when he returned. The pursing of her lips and the pleat between her eyebrows made her indecision clear. If he didn't want her to walk out, he'd better start talking.

He nodded toward her room. "You have your own bathroom and there's a lock on the bedroom door. Not that you need it. I don't go where I'm not invited."

While she chewed on that, he retrieved his case, letting the door to the hall close and shut out the rest of the world. After depositing his bag in his bedroom, Carter opened the wine and waited for Phoebe's next move. Did she have the guts to stay? Or would she insist on another room?

Wariness clouded her eyes. He offered her a glass of wine and she hesitated before accepting. "You didn't used to be devious, Carter."

No, he'd been a puppet with his strings securely wrapped around Phoebe's slender fingers. "This isn't devious. It's efficient. I don't want to waste time calling your room to tell you I've returned or to see if you're ready."

The first step toward getting her to unwind was losing the gray pin-striped power suit she'd worn for the flight, and while he'd prefer to strip it from her personally, he suspected she'd object. "Did you bring jeans and sneakers?"

"As you ordered? Yes."

"Change. Eat. We leave in ninety minutes."

Her stance straightened and her lips thinned. Strategical error. He should have phrased that as a request rather than an order. Phoebe, he'd noticed, had a problem with orders.

"Where are we going?"

Her eyes used to brim with excitement and anticipation when she asked that question. Today he saw wariness and suspicion. "It's a surprise."

Her brows lowered. "I don't like surprises."

"I've noticed, but I guarantee you'll like this one."

Phoebe strode from the room. Carter exhaled a frustrated breath. *Patience. Don't rush the plan. You have five days and four nights to accomplish your goal. She'll be relaxed and receptive in no time.*

Within ten minutes Carter had unpacked and returned to the common area. Forty minutes later he'd snacked on crackers and cheese, verified a cab would be available at the specified time, confirmed tomorrow's tickets and rental car and taken twelve laps around the room.

Was Phoebe avoiding him? Women hadn't avoided him since he'd bulked up and gained confidence. His money guaranteed he'd never be without a date when he wanted one. Women came to him. He didn't have to chase. Except for Phoebe. Disgusted, he downed the rest of his wine and deposited the glass on the table. He'd rather have a beer than this pricey stuff.

His time could be better spent reviewing the job his team would begin Friday morning. He pulled the file from his brief-case and opened it, but his thoughts remained focused on the woman holed up on the other side of the closed door instead of the elaborate computer security system CyberSniper would install over the weekend. Twenty minutes later he admitted defeat, crossed the room and rapped on her door.

The panel slowly opened. "Yes?"

Phoebe's starched cotton blouse and stiff new jeans looked as crisp as her suit, and she hadn't let down her hair, but her worn sneakers weren't the same ones that had rubbed blisters on her heels last week. Those broken-in, slightly battered shoes gave him hope that his mission had a chance. Some part of her still knew how to unwind and get comfortable.

He checked his watch. "You didn't eat anything and it's time to go."

"I needed to work."

Beyond her shoulder he spotted her laptop and an assort-ment of neatly stacked files on the desk beside the empty wineglass. She'd rather work than spend time with him? The knowledge stung. "When I'm here, your time is mine."

Her shoulders squared and her eyes glinted with irritation. His words had a possessive tone he hadn't intended, but he'd be damned if he'd brought her down here only to be ignored. And he wouldn't apologize. He'd apologized enough twelve years ago for not being able to afford the kinds of dates she deserved.

"Let's go."

Carter gave the cabbie the street address. He wanted to maintain the suspense as long as possible. Back in his poorer days he and Phoebe had attended as many free events as possible, including the university football games. Although it was a different sport season and the tickets in his pocket certainly hadn't been free, the relaxed atmosphere would be the same.

The taxi driver took the curves too fast and darted in and out of traffic with total disregard for the other vehicles on the road. Carter had long since learned to ignore the perils of a taxi ride, but this time each swerve flung Phoebe against his shoulder. Each bump electrified him, and her scent surrounded him. The flush on her cheeks led him to conclude that she wasn't immune to the contact, either. Good.

"Not used to cabs?"

She clutched the front of the seat with white-knuckled fingers. "My grandfather has a car service."

He wouldn't let the reminder of their differences sidetrack his plan for the evening.

The cabbie pulled to the curb. Carter paid him and helped Phoebe from the vehicle. She withdrew her hand as soon as she reached the sidewalk. "Where are we?"

"Are you familiar with Atlanta?"

"Only the convention center."

Carter smiled, cupped her elbow and guided her along the sidewalk.

"Carter, you didn't answer my question."

"No, I didn't." The number of pedestrians increased as they neared Turner Field. He threaded his fingers through hers to keep from getting separated. It irritated him that the press of her palm against his was enough to overload his circuits. They turned the corner and the crowd thickened. Phoebe stopped, but the throng kept pushing, forcing her snugly against him.

"We're going to a Braves' game?"

"Yes." Carter hooked an arm around her waist and guided her forward. Every shuffled step and shift of her weight against him fired sparks in his blood.

"Do you know how long it's been since I attended a ball game?" She didn't give him time to reply. "Remember that homecoming football game we attended back in school? It was cold and we had to huddle in a blanket. And your hands were so cold against my—" She bit her lip and looked away.

Against her breasts. He remembered. The game hadn't been their only entertainment that afternoon.

"This should be fun. Thank you." The sparkle of excitement in her eyes captured him, but the smile on her lips sucked him in. The urge to kiss her right here, right now, in the middle of the jostling horde, surged through him. Instead he reached into his pocket, pulled out his tiny digital camera and snapped a picture.

Phoebe frowned. "I wish you wouldn't keep doing that."

He distracted her by asking, "Know anything about the team?"

"I've met a few of the players at political functions."

She'd met players while he was happy to be a season ticket holder. Another reminder that the senator's granddaughter and the military brat didn't move in the same circles. But for the next five days they would, and then Carter would let her go. This time, he vowed, Phoebe would be the only one with regrets.

Phoebe couldn't remember when she'd last raised her voice. Loud voices and arguments brought back painful memories of the final time she'd seen her parents. But tonight she'd yelled plenty and loved it.

Tremendously relaxed from the vodka-laced frozen lemonades she'd consumed at the ballpark along with an unhealthy array of junk food, she floated into the hotel suite with a big smile on her face and Carter on her heels. Big, strong Carter, who had kept her from getting lost in the post-game exodus by banding a muscular arm around her waist. Carter, who smelled too good and looked too good, had been a very patient teacher to this brand-new baseball fan. By the seventh inning stretch Phoebe had been cheering for the home team and singing "Take Me Out to the Ball Game" with the rest of the crowd.

Moderation in all things. Oops, her grandmother's words echoed in Phoebe's head one spiked lemonade too late. She'd best carry herself off to bed before she did something she'd regret, such as kiss the handsome, heartbreaking lug beside her for reminding her how to have fun. Phoebe hadn't had a lot of fun before she'd met Carter or since their breakup. He'd shown her how to play twelve years ago and today he'd given her a much-needed reminder not to take life so seriously. Too bad she couldn't use the lesson once she returned home. In D.C. everything was serious business.

Tomorrow while Carter was working she'd do her penance in the hotel gym for the extra calories she'd consumed during the game. Tonight… She looked up at the smile tugging Carter's lips and the camera in his hand and lost her train of thought. Oh yeah, tonight she needed to stay out of trouble. She extracted herself from his embrace and wobbled a safe distance away. "I wish you'd keep your camera in your pocket."

"I never go anywhere without it."

"I noticed."

"Want me to call room service for a pot of coffee?"

Phoebe blinked and shifted her gaze from the intriguing movement of his lips back to his eyes. Was he laughing at her? "You think I'm drunk?"

He arched a brow. "Close enough."

"I never drink. Except wine. And I'm not drunk. I'm just…relaxed."

"I can tell." A dimple appeared in his cheek.

"I only had three drinks in three hours. If I drink coffee now, I'll never get to sleep." She pursed her lips and wished he'd quit looking at her as if he found her terribly amusing. Phoebe Lancaster Drew was never amusing. Professional. Yes. Poised. Certainly. Funny. No. Absolutely not.

"Would you like for me to arrange for a wake-up call? I won't be here to get you up tomorrow morning."

"You won't?"

"I have to take a trip to the job site. I'll come back for you at noon."

She ought to be relieved that she wouldn't have to face him over breakfast. But perversely she wasn't. "Where are we going tomorrow?"

"Another surprise. You'll enjoy it. Promise." He winked and her stomach bottomed out.

"As much as I enjoyed tonight? I had a wonderful time, Carter. Thank you." A lock of hair fell over her eye. She puffed a breath, trying to blow it out of the way.

Carter closed the distance between them, lifted his hand and tucked the strand behind her ear. Phoebe shivered at the touch of his fingers and closed her eyes against the need to press her cheek into his palm. She heard him inhale sharply and then his lips touched hers. Softly, insistently, he incited her senses to riot with sipping kisses and swipes of his tongue.

Her head spun. Her muscles weakened and her heart pounded. Phoebe clutched his biceps and hung on as their tongues danced. The distance between them vanished. His hard body pressed her soft curves, making her breasts and that spot low in her tummy ache. Phoebe wound her arms around his waist and sighed into his mouth.

Carter caught her upper arms and held her away. "Time for bed."

She blinked up at him, trying to make the jump from feeling deliciously warm and sexy to common sense. When he held her like this, kissed her like that, it was hard to remember why she didn't want to get involved with him again. Oh, yeah. He'd broken her heart. "I'm not going to sleep with you."

"Alone." Carter's clipped voice and stern expression banished what was left of her intoxication. He released her, retrieved two bottles of water from the room refrigerator and shoved them into her hands. "Drink these before you pass out. If you don't pump some liquid through your system you're going to feel like hell in the morning. Good night, Phoebe."

He turned on his heel, entered his own bedroom and closed the door with a solid *thunk*.

She wanted to call him back.

What was wrong with her? Why did she keep making the same mistakes over and over again? Hadn't she learned anything from her painful past? Phoebe pressed the cold bottles against her hot cheeks.

No more alcohol.

No more kisses.

No more getting caught up in the past and letting down her guard. Otherwise she'd be in for another broken heart.

Wuss. Wimp. Fool. Carter punctuated each self-directed barb with a lift of the weights in the hotel's empty workout room at 4:00 a.m. He'd had Phoebe exactly where he wanted her last night. And he'd let her go.

She'd been willing. The pulse fluttering wildly at the base of her neck and her ravenous kisses had been an invitation to do more than kiss her. An invitation he'd refused.

You're getting soft, Jones.

He wanted Phoebe, but he didn't want her drunk or even slightly tipsy when he sought his pleasure. He wanted her one hundred percent aware of who she'd taken into her body and one hundred percent with him.

Few missions are accomplished without a little compromise.

But Carter refused to compromise on fighting fair. He'd win this battle with his brain not with dirty tricks.

His muscles ached and his knee protested the additional weigh he'd added to his workout in an attempt to exorcise his frustration and self-directed anger. It would serve him right if he ended up back under the knife after this stunt.

He wiped the sweat from his face with the hem of his T-shirt. Next time he'd succeed. Next time he'd lay a kiss on Phoebe Lancaster Drew that would soak her panties. Next time she'd be sober and nothing would come between him and the success of Operation Seduction.

Carter returned to the hotel room, showered and dressed. On his way out of the suite he detoured, easing open Phoebe's bedroom door. *Just to make sure she's all right.* He took in her wrinkled sheets, her sleep-flushed face and the tumbled dark hair spread across her white pillowcase and clenched his teeth against a slam of desire so strong it tempted him to forget the client who'd paid well for his time and expertise this weekend, crawl in bed and awaken Phoebe with his hands and mouth.

He could have spent part of the night in that bed with her if he'd had a few less scruples, but he didn't want to see regret in her eyes when her pulse slowed and the sweat cooled on her skin. He wanted her still wanting him when he said goodbye—the same way he'd wanted her when she'd ended their relationship. He pulled out his camera and snapped a shot.

The empty water bottles stood on the bedside table. Good. The last thing he wanted was a hungover date. Last night he'd loosened her straitjacket of propriety.

Today he intended to make Phoebe scream.

* * *

"Again. I want to ride again," Phoebe croaked in a voice made hoarse by screaming her way through the corkscrew turns and breathtaking drops of the roller coaster.

Carter shook his head. "We've ridden this one four times already. Let's try a different ride."

"But I like this one." It shamed Phoebe to admit her sense of adventure was limited to familiar things. She knew she could handle *this* roller coaster, but she wasn't sure about the amusement park's other thrill rides.

"Phoebe, you weren't keen on this one when I suggested—"

She held up a hand. "You didn't suggest. You ordered."

"My point is, you didn't think you'd like this ride and you did. It's time to expand your horizons."

"Did you know that I have never been to an amusement park before today? Let's walk around and see the shows. Do they have exhibits?" She took off toward a gaming booth.

Carter caught her hand and tugged her back to his side. "Phoebe."

Her name in that gruff, you're-not-bluffing-me voice, made Phoebe cringe. Carter had always been able to read her. She resented that he still had that skill when she'd lost the ability to see past his poker face. His long, warm fingers enclosing hers had a strong effect on her stomach—not unlike the plunge of the roller coaster over its steepest hill. She pulled free. "If I get sick, it's your fault."

"I'll take my chances, and I'll buy you a couple of chili dogs afterward."

She shook her head. "I had two at the ball game yesterday. I need to limit my junk food."

Carter's intense blue gaze glided over her neat lavender polo shirt, tailored navy shorts, bare legs and back again with the potent impact of a lingering caress. Heat flared in his eyes and a corresponding flicker licked through Phoebe. She folded her arms over her breasts to cover her telling response.

"You have nothing to worry about."

She had plenty to worry about if he could make her knees quiver with nothing more than a slow look. *Toughen up, Phoebe.* "Thank you."

"Enough stalling. Let's go."

Five hours later Phoebe's throat hurt and she probably had a sunburn despite the liberal application of sunscreen and wearing the goofy hat Carter had won for her, but she hadn't had this much fun in ages. Correction. She'd never had this much fun. And to think she'd almost refused to get out of the rental car when Carter had parked outside the amusement park gates.

If anybody in the crowded park recognized her, they hadn't infringed on her space. Here she wasn't Senator Wilton Lancaster's granddaughter, hostess and speech writer, the woman always standing behind his right shoulder when the press snapped a picture. Today she was just another visitor having a fun-filled day, and the only camera she had to worry about was Carter's.

Exhausted, she plopped down on the end of a bench with less grace than she'd ever displayed in her life, but the constant rush and ebb of adrenaline had exhausted her. "I'm having a good time."

"You sound surprised." Carter eased down beside her in the middle of the seat, leaned back and splayed his legs. His thigh pressed hers.

The wrought-iron arm of the bench blocked Phoebe's escape. She swallowed and tried to focus on something other than the heat of his bare skin against hers and the tickle of awareness caused by his dark, wiry leg hairs. "It's been a while since I've had time for fun and games."

"You should make time. All work and no pl—"

"Please spare me the clichés. Maybe after the election I'll have time." But it wouldn't happen. Granddad would be elected and her workload would increase exponentially. Visits like this one to the park or last night's ball game would require a bevy of secret service agents and become front-page news.

Carter stretched his arms along the back of the bench, encompassing Phoebe in his long reach. Closing his eyes against the glare of the setting sun on their faces, he rested his head against the tree behind the bench.

The unexpected urge to lean against his broad chest tugged at her. Years ago Carter had held her and made her feel secure when being away from home and from her grandparents for the first time had made Phoebe anxious. But that was then. Carter wasn't the same man at thirty-three that he'd been at twenty-one. And she certainly wasn't the same shy girl.

She sat forward and turned her head to study the changes in him. Dark stubble coated his chin. Fine lines fanned out from his eyes and a half dozen gray hairs mingled with the dark strands at his temples. The boy she'd known had become a man—a man to be reckoned with if her research was accurate. And a hero. He'd saved that young girl's life.

Although Carter hadn't ever opened up about his deepest fears and desires twelve years ago, Phoebe had known he'd had something to prove. Had he succeeded?

He owned a stately home and a company of which he could be proud. She, on the other hand, still lived with her grandfather, dividing her time between the state capital and the nation's capital. Most people believed she had the home and career of her dreams. They were wrong. Phoebe had never wanted to live the public life that had exasperated her mother enough to make her elope with a construction worker she'd met during the remodeling of the Lancaster estate.

One of Carter's lids lifted slightly. He observed her through the slit. "Only one roller coaster left."

Phoebe's stomach muscles clenched. "I've worked up quite an appetite. Let's have dinner. Didn't the food court on the other side of the park have vegetable stir-fry?"

"I'll try to win you the stuffed bear you wanted if you'll ride that." He eased upright, rested his arm along her shoulders and turned her toward a roller coaster that not only plunged and swung the riders forward; it repeated the terrifying ride backward.

Phoebe blamed her sudden breathlessness on fear of the ride rather than Carter's touch. *Pure political whitewash.* She scooted forward on the seat and he lowered his arm, allowing Phoebe to focus on the issue at hand. How could she anticipate trouble and brace herself for it if she couldn't see it coming? No, she wasn't riding the backward ride. "I don't have anywhere to keep the bear."

"Then ride it for a photo. I'll give you one tonight."

Horrified, she gaped at him and hugged herself against a sudden chilling reminder. Once again Carter had made her forget who she was and what her position entailed. Hadn't he taught her that letting her guard down could have disastrous consequences?

Suddenly conscious of her sunburned, windblown and unkempt appearance, she yanked the silly hat off her head and tried to smooth her hair back into its French twist. The tangles told her it was a lost cause.

"You have them here? In Atlanta? Or here in the park?"

"At the hotel."

She pressed a hand to her chest as if she could slow her

racing heart with the pressure. "You left the pictures in the hotel where they could be stolen?"

"You'd rather I bring them along and have them fall out of my pocket when we're upside down on that?" His nod indicated the roller coaster they'd ridden moments ago.

A headache chiseled its way through her temple. "No, but…"

"The photos are secure."

How could she have forgotten even for one moment why she was here? "I want to leave."

"Phoebe—"

"Now, Carter." Without waiting for his reply, she vaulted to her feet and headed toward the exit at a speed-walking pace.

Carter caught up with her, grabbed her hand and pulled her to a stop in the middle of the wide sidewalk. Patrons parted and detoured around them. Nervous about attracting attention, Phoebe glanced left and then right. She tried to extract her hand without causing a scene, but Carter wouldn't release her. He led her out of traffic to a secluded area between an ice-cream stand and a fence and cupped her shoulders, holding her captive until she met his gaze.

"Haven't you figured out yet that I'm not going to embarrass you with the pictures?"

"You wouldn't be embarrassing me, Carter. I am responsible for my own actions, and I've embarrassed myself with my behavior. I should have thought about the possible repercussions before selfishly indulging my whims." *Again,* she added silently.

Carter's lips tightened. His hands lowered. He didn't try to conceal his disgust. "Heaven forbid the senator find out you're human."

"You don't understand."

"Make me understand, Phoebe."

He hadn't cared about her loyalty to her grandfather twelve years ago. Today wouldn't be any different, and she didn't have the time or energy right now to compose a speech that would sway an unreceptive audience.

"I'd like to leave. I have a headache."

"Running?"

Phoebe halted midturn. "From what?"

"From what's between us."

She paused, trying to gather her scattered thoughts. *The best defense is offense.* "I'm sorry if you've misinterpreted my actions."

"I'm not misreading anything. You're as aware of and curious about the sparks between us as I am."

The accuracy of his words winded her. "You're mistaken."

"Am I? I don't think so, sugar." He dragged a fingertip from her shoulder to her elbow and then along the inside of her forearm to her palm.

Phoebe silently cursed the shiver that proved his point. "I have sunburn. My skin is sensitive."

"Your skin always has been sensitive—to my touch, that is." He brushed the backs of his knuckles along her jaw and cupped her nape. Alarm bells clanged loudly in Phoebe's mind, but they were in a public place. What could he do?

A moment later she was sorry she'd underestimated him as his lips captured hers in a kiss so unanticipated and untamed her muscles locked. His mouth opened, parting hers and devouring her. Torn between pushing him away and pulling him closer, Phoebe alternately flattened her hands and clenched her fists against his chest.

Why him? Why did Carter Jones have the power to arouse her and to make her wish she were some nobody and not the future president's granddaughter? And why did she have to keep telling him no? She stiffened. Because she had too much to lose. He'd break her, and in the process cost her the only family she had left.

He lifted his head. Phoebe reluctantly opened her eyes and looked around to see how many people had witnessed her becoming putty in Carter's big hands, but Carter's broad shoulders blocked her from onlookers.

His jaw muscles bunched as if he were grinding his teeth. "Let's go."

Six

If he'd made as many mistakes during his military service as he'd made with Phoebe, he'd be dead.

Carter had miscalculated again, and Phoebe's barricades were back and fortified. Did he have any chance of pulling this mission out of the latrine?

An insistent buzzing penetrated his black mood—not that he'd been able to concentrate worth a damn since returning from the amusement park. He tossed the file folder onto the coffee table, rose and tracked the noise to Phoebe's room. He tapped on the slightly ajar door. No response. Pushing back the panel, he stepped into the room and spotted her cell phone vibrating its way across the top of the dresser. The sound of running water from the bathroom told him Phoebe was in the shower—not an image he needed if he wanted to concentrate on complex schematics.

The phone teetered off the edge of the dresser. Carter

Get FREE BOOKS and a FREE GIFT when you play the...

LAS VEGAS
GAME

Just scratch off the gold box with a coin. Then check below to see the gifts you get!

YES! I have scratched off the gold box. Please send me my **2 FREE BOOKS** and **gift for which I qualify.** I understand that I am under no obligation to purchase any books as explained on the back of this card.

326 SDL D7Y5   225 SDL D7YV

FIRST NAME   LAST NAME

ADDRESS

APT.#   CITY

STATE/PROV.   ZIP/POSTAL CODE   (S-D-06/05)

7	7	7	Worth TWO FREE BOOKS plus a BONUS Mystery Gift!
			Worth TWO FREE BOOKS!
			TRY AGAIN!

www.eHarlequin.com

Offer limited to one per household and not valid to current Silhouette Desire® subscribers. All orders subject to approval.

► DETACH AND MAIL CARD TODAY! ►

The Silhouette Reader Service™ — Here's how it works:

Accepting your 2 free books and mystery gift places you under no obligation to buy anything. You may keep the books and gift and return the shipping statement marked "cancel." If you do not cancel, about a month later we'll send you 6 additional books and bill you just $3.80 each in the U.S., or $4.47 each in Canada, plus 25¢ shipping & handling per book and applicable taxes if any.* That's the complete price and — compared to cover prices of $4.50 each in the U.S. and $5.25 each in Canada — it's quite a bargain! You may cancel at any time, but if you choose to continue, every month we'll send you 6 more books, which you may either purchase at the discount price or return to us and cancel your subscription.

*Terms and prices subject to change without notice. Sales tax applicable in N.Y. Canadian residents will be charged applicable provincial taxes and GST. Credit or Debit balances in a customer's account(s) may be offset by any other outstanding balance owed by or to the customer.

lunged forward and caught it before it hit the floor. He glanced at the Caller ID display on the phone. *Daniel Wisenaut.* Who was he and why was he calling Phoebe? Carter hit the talk button. "Hello?"

"Pardon me. I must have dialed the wrong number," a male voice replied.

The hairs on the back of Carter's neck rose. Was the man Phoebe's lover? "Are you trying to reach Phoebe?"

"Yes. Who is this?"

Carter considered his options. The caller offered him the perfect opportunity to make his dates with Phoebe public knowledge, but he didn't know who was on the other end. *Never trust an unidentified enemy.* "Phoebe can't come to the phone. I'll have her return your call."

"Who is this," he repeated, "and where are you? I tried the house and no one answered."

The water shut off in the bathroom. A picture of Phoebe naked and wet paraded through Carter's mind. He ground his teeth against the testosterone surging through his blood. "Phoebe will tell you if she thinks you need to know."

Carter punched the end button.

The bathroom door opened. A cloud of steam preceded Phoebe from the room. In the moments before she spotted him, Carter soaked up every detail from her dark, wet hair and sun-kissed nose and cheeks to the way the white hotel robe clung to her damp curves. The flowery scent of her shampoo or soap or whatever it was drifted over him.

Phoebe lifted her head, locked gazes with him and froze. Her expression switched from calm to guarded in the blink of an eye. "Get out of my room."

He offered the cell phone. "You had a call."

Her eyes widened in horror. She pulled the robe tighter

with one hand and snatched the phone from him with the other. "You answered my phone? Was it my grandfather?"

"Caller ID said Daniel Wisenaut."

Her pained expression made his gut clench. "My grandfather's personal assistant. You might as well have dialed my grandfather directly."

"I thought you'd want to know who called."

"I have voice mail."

He shrugged. Most people did, but most didn't have the sudden urge to mark their territory that he'd had. Jealousy? Nah. Phoebe might not be his for the long haul, but she was his for the weekend. "Dinner's on its way up."

She closed her eyes and took a deep breath. The rise and fall of her braless breasts behind the robe riveted him. "I need to get dressed and then call Daniel. Something could be wrong with my grandfather."

He should take consolation in the knowledge that she didn't want to talk to Daniel while she was naked. But he didn't. The man had her personal number—a number Carter didn't have. And he didn't want Wisenaut intruding on his evening with Phoebe and erasing the progress he'd made over the past two days.

As if on cue, a knock sounded at the sitting room door. "He didn't say it was urgent. I'll let in room service. Join me, Phoebe, before your stir-fry congeals. Please," he added when she hesitated.

"I need to dress."

He allowed himself the pleasure of inspecting her damp, flushed body once more. "If you insist, but don't go to any trouble on my account. You look fine to me."

When he again met her gaze she held it for several heartbeats and his pulse kicked up a notch. He noted her dilated pupils and parted lips as she breathed a little faster, but instead

f inviting him to stay, she clutched her phone to her chest
and inclined her head toward the door in a clear dismissal.

An invitation to serve her dinner in bed obviously wouldn't
be forthcoming tonight. But tomorrow was another day.

Phoebe stared at her cell phone the way she would a hiss-
ing snake. Daniel was the last person she wanted to talk to tonight. But what if something was wrong with her grandfather?
Surely Daniel would have told Carter if this were an emergency? She had to call. But first she pulled a dark red, scoop-
necked dress in a crushproof fabric over her head and stepped
into her pumps. After running a comb through her towel-
dried hair, she reluctantly picked up the phone. Daniel an-
wered on the first ring.

"It's Phoebe returning your call."

"Where are you and who answered your phone?"

She balked at his peevish tone. "Is something wrong with
Granddad?"

"Other than being in a snit because he wants the special
interest file and you're not at home to fax it? No."

Her tense muscles loosened. Her grandfather had elected
to take good ol' Danny Boy along on his male-only campaign
strategy trip but had left Phoebe behind—a fact that irritated
her immensely on many levels but relieved her on others. As
her grandfather's speech writer she'd be expected to turn his
campaign platform into something palatable for the public,
and there were certain policies even she couldn't sell that
needed to be downplayed. On the other hand, Phoebe de-
tested the endless rounds of golf and political back-scratch-
ing. Decisions that could be made in a matter of minutes
stretched into a marathon of bipartisan dancing on the putting
greens. For an efficient person like her that seemed like a vast
amount of wasted time.

Phoebe squared her shoulders. "I'm entitled to a vacation.

"With whom?" Daniel repeated.

If she told him, he'd run straight to her grandfather, an
Carter would be under full investigation within a matter c
minutes. Not a desired outcome. "A friend."

"A male friend? The senator won't be happy." No doub
Daniel would be spilling the information in hopes of gainin
approval points for being a snitch. He'd never thought of any
one but himself.

Phoebe expelled an exasperated breath. "What do you—

His ominous laugh made Phoebe's skin prickle in a flesh
crawling way. "Or perhaps he will be. Wilton had begun t
suspect you were gay. Knowing you're with a man will be
huge relief in many respects despite the possible politica
backlash."

Shock seized Phoebe's vocal cords, quickly followed by
hot flush of anger. "And who planted that ridiculous assump
tion in his head, Daniel, since I've never given him any rea
son to believe that?"

The rumor could have originated from only one source—
from someone who hadn't wanted to accept any of the blam
for their broken engagement. Daniel. Phoebe often had fe
as if her ex-fiancé were trying to come between her and he
grandfather. This only confirmed her suspicions. How dar
Daniel try to break up what little family she had left? But
he had poisoned the senator's mind with this sordid lie,
could explain why her grandfather had stopped throwin
young lawyers at her after she ended her engagement tw
years ago.

"Phoebe, we both know you're not a highly sexual woman

Daniel's denigrating words stung like alcohol poured o
an open wound. He wouldn't call her asexual if he knew abou
her scandalous past or how badly she ached right now for Ca

ter to stroke her body with more than his hot gaze. These past two days of fun in the sun had reminded her why she had fallen for Carter years ago and, therefore, increased her desire for him.

Unlike her feelings for Daniel... He had been everything her grandfather wanted in a grandson-in-law. Because her grandfather liked and respected Daniel, Phoebe had tried very hard to be happy with him. After they'd become engaged she'd even gone to bed with him. The encounters had been embarrassing and unfulfilling, but since she wasn't looking for the love and passion she'd shared with Carter, Phoebe had convinced herself the relationship could work. Eventually she'd admitted something crucial was missing from the tepid association, something that wasn't going to improve over time, and she'd broached Daniel with her doubts. He'd laughed and informed her that he wasn't in love with her, either, but with his experience and her pedigree they'd make an unbeatable political duo and a fine president and first lady.

His answer had given Phoebe the excuse she'd needed to break the engagement. She'd never wanted to live in the Pennsylvania Avenue fish bowl. Ironically she could very well end up in the White House with her grandfather. Daniel hadn't taken the news well, but she'd had no idea he'd concoct such a far-fetched tale for her grandfather. But then again, she shouldn't be surprised. Daniel was doing what he did best— looking out for himself and protecting his job. Too bad she hadn't known that before becoming engaged to him.

"Face it," he continued. "You've never had a lasting relationship with a man, and in bed you were...well, I'll be polite and say, disinterested."

Shame burned her skin. Anger set her teeth on edge. She felt dirty and wanted another shower. With a few carefully chosen words about her past she could set Daniel straight, but she kept her secret for fear he'd use it against her. "Perhaps it was the company."

He tsked. "Bitter barbs are out of character for you, Phoebe. You would have made an amazing first lady. So poised. So gracious. Unless you come to your senses soon I'll have to take the White House without you."

"Be my guest, Daniel. I have the special interest notes on my laptop. I'll e-mail them to Granddad tonight."

She disconnected and paced the length of her room. For years she'd tried to live above reproach and out of the D.C. gossips' eyes, but the only things she'd gained from her celibacy were loneliness and now a false accusation of being a lesbian. Her grandfather must be horrified. He wasn't the most tolerant sort, and gay rights registered nowhere on his personal Richter scale. She'd have to set him straight and that wasn't a conversation either of them would enjoy. Would he even believe her? Daniel could be quite convincing.

Too agitated to face Carter, Phoebe booted up her computer and sent the files. When she'd calmed down sufficiently, she took a deep breath and opened her door.

Two steps into the room Phoebe halted. She wasn't up to this tonight.

Carter had set the scene for seduction. He'd extinguished the sitting room lights and pulled back the curtains to reveal a breathtaking view of nighttime Atlanta. The only illumination in the room came from two tall tapers on the table in front of the window. If she turned on the lamps to kill the mood, then she'd have to close the curtains to the view, and she needed all the distraction from her dinner companion she could get.

Carter rose from the shadows of the sofa. When he'd come into her room earlier she'd been too stunned to take in his attire. He'd showered, shaved and combed back his hair. His cologne teased her senses, and his white dress shirt, unbuttoned at the neck, revealed a tuft of dark curls. Black pants hugged his lean hips. He was easily the most attractive man Phoebe had ever encountered.

"You look beautiful, Phoebe." If that was a line, he could win voter points for credibility.

How could he arouse her with mere words when Daniel hadn't been able to with his touch? "Thank you. You shouldn't have waited. Your dinner will be cold."

"I'd prefer to have your company while I eat."

He knew all the right things to say, but at the moment her ego needed the balm, so she didn't call him on it. Determined to block the unpleasant phone conversation from her thoughts, Phoebe made her way to the table and lifted the lids on their dinners. The scent of teriyaki sauce and roasted vegetables rose on a cloud of steam, making her mouth water. Carter had ordered a steak with all the trimmings for himself.

He seated her. His knuckles brushed against her spine as he swept her hair clear of the chair back. Her skin tingled and her breath hitched. He lifted the wine bottle, but she covered her glass. "No wine for me tonight. I'll stick with water."

He settled across the table from her. She avoided his watchful gaze by sampling a bite of her meal. The flavorful spices and crisp vegetables mingled on her tongue. "Delicious."

"Good." They ate in silence for several moments. "Who is Daniel Wisenaut—besides your grandfather's personal assistant?"

Phoebe nearly choked on her water. She set down the glass with an unsteady hand. Her appetite vanished. "Why do you ask?"

"The expression on your face when I told you he'd called."

Why lie? If he asked around, anyone could tell him. "Daniel is my ex-fiancé."

Carter's jaw shifted. "What happened?"

"Nothing. He's perfect—exactly the kind of man my grandfather wants me to marry."

Carter silently held her gaze, his expression revealing none of his thoughts. "Then why didn't you?"

She considered politely evading his question, but given the phone call, she wasn't feeling particularly charitable toward Daniel at the moment. "He was more concerned with courting my grandfather than me."

"He's a jackass."

His swift defense warmed and disarmed her. "Yes, but a politically savvy one. He wants to be president one day, and I have no doubt he'll succeed."

"Did your grandfather know Wisenaut was using you to climb the Washington political ladder?"

Her cheeks burned. Phoebe wished she could blame the heat on her slight sunburn instead of Carter's accurate summation. Daniel had found the weak link in penetrating the protective enclave around Washington's most influential senator. She was ashamed to admit that weak link had been her. "I never told him."

"And now Wisenaut works for the senator."

"He became Granddad's assistant before I ended the engagement. Daniel is good at his job, and Granddad likes him."

"Did you love him?"

She paused, unwilling to reveal her vow to never fall in love again because it would empower Carter with the knowledge of how badly he'd hurt her in the past. "Good marriages are based on more than just sentiment and lust. I thought I could learn to care for him over time."

"You're willing to settle?" His accusatory words fired like bullets.

"I've tried love, if you remember, and it didn't work out." She regretted her peevish outburst immediately. Pressing her fingertips to the headache pecking at her temple, she ducked her head and tried to smother the festering hurt Daniel's barbs had caused.

"I remember."

Carter's softly spoken words squeezed her heart. She met his solemn gaze. "Tonight Daniel told me he thought I was gay, and evidently he's informed my grandfather of his conclusion." Her brief laugh held no mirth. "They have no idea how wrong they are."

"Are they?"

She stared at Carter in shock. Was he playing devil's advocate the way he used to or was he serious? Had he also found her a dud in bed? No, no he hadn't. She knew that for a fact. Didn't she? Or had he been so grateful to finally lose his virginity that any woman would have done? Had the women he'd made love with since been better in bed? Her doubts stung like wasps.

"For God's sake, Carter, you know better. We've been together. I've never wanted a woman in that way."

"In what way?" He pinned her with an unblinking stare.

Unable to look away from his vivid blue eyes, Phoebe bit the inside of her lip. Honesty would land her in very deep water. At the moment she was too shaken to care. She needed to know if he'd also found her lacking. Could she handle the consequences of being candid? "Sexually. In the way I want you."

His nostrils flared as he inhaled sharply.

She held up her hands. "I'm sorry. I shouldn't have said that. I laid the ground rules and I've broken—"

"But you did say it." His jaw muscles flexed. Carter laid his napkin on the table and rose with deliberate intent.

Phoebe's heart pounded and her lungs ceased to function. She crushed her napkin in her hands. "This isn't wise."

"Why not? We're two straight, consenting, unattached adults who find each other attractive. I'm clean. You?" The low rumble of his voice made her shiver.

It took a moment for his meaning to sink in. "Y-yes."

He stopped behind her chair and Phoebe's entire body clenched in anticipation, *in dread* of his next move. The warmth of his hands settled on her shoulders. His thumbs worked over the knotted muscles of her neck. Her head fell forward and her eyes closed.

Stop him.

Why?

He'll hurt you.

A battle with her conscience raged inside her, but Phoebe couldn't fight the magic in Carter's touch. Tension swirled in her abdomen, winding tighter with his every move. Heat pooled in her lap. Each hair on her head became a pleasure receptor as he dragged his fingers through the strands, massaging her scalp the way he had years ago when she'd had migraines. He'd always known what to do to relieve her stress.

Her headache faded and something much more dangerous took its place. Hunger. A hunger she hadn't experienced in over a decade. No other man had ever made her feel this way.

She didn't want to say no tonight.

An unwise decision. One you'll undoubtedly regret.

Thirty-year-old women have affairs all the time.

But not you.

Who will know? The argument with her conscience continued.

Carter stroked her chest above the scooped neck of her dress with a feather-light touch. His scent, his nearness, overwhelmed her. Her fight-or-flight response yielded to softened muscles and building heat. Phoebe's nipples tightened into pearls. He shifted behind her and then his lips brushed the juncture of skin between her neck and shoulders. She gasped as a lightning bolt of desire shot through her and covered his hands with her own.

"Carter—"

"Shh." His teeth caught her earlobe and hers clamped down on a moan. Sensation rippled in the wake of his caresses over her shoulders and upper arms. He grazed her with his lips, laved her skin with his tongue, nipped her with his teeth. Sparks of pleasure danced through her, energizing her, heating her, moistening her.

Carter tasted his way across her nape to the opposite shoulder. Phoebe lifted a hand to push him away, but her fingers ended up curled in his springy hair, holding him close.

He cupped her breasts, kneading them and plucking at the sensitive tips. She let her head fall back and Carter captured her mouth, kissing her as if he intended to devour her where she sat. Seconds later he pulled her from her seat and aligned her against his body. The hot length of him burned against her belly and her blood gathered at the pressure point.

Light-headed with need, she swayed against him and scrambled for coherent thought. "Carter, if we do this…it can only be here. In Atlanta. When I get home I—I don't have time to drive back and forth between D.C. and North Carolina anymore, and I can't afford the negative publicity of an affair."

His gaze bored into hers. The fire in his eyes took on a steely glint. "Three days. That'll be enough for you?"

It would have to be. Her pulse drummed in her ears. "Yes."

His fingers tangled in her hair and tugged, angling her head for one deep, spine-melting kiss after another. Phoebe twined her arms around his waist and grasped his belt as the strength left her knees. He hissed when her fingertips slipped beneath the leather and retaliated by thrusting his tongue into her mouth, mimicking what he intended to do with his body.

One big hand raked her back and cupped her bottom, sliding her along the thigh he'd thrust between hers. Phoebe shamelessly followed his lead, rubbing against him and creating a conflagration deep inside. The fabric of her dress was in the way. She wanted his hands on her skin and hers on his. With a yank and a tug she pulled his shirttail from his waistband and found the hot, supple flesh beneath.

He shivered when she dragged her fingertips across his lower back, and Phoebe reveled in her ability to pull a response from him.

Her breasts ached against the wall of his chest, but the contact wasn't enough. She leaned back and tackled the buttons of his shirt with trembling fingers. Her common sense rallied at the sight of his chest bared to the waistband of his slacks.

What was she doing?

With her hand hovering an inch away from his skin, Phoebe hesitated. Could she make love with Carter without falling in love with him all over again?

Carter captured her hand and pressed it over his rapidly beating heart. Phoebe's pulse rate tripled.

Yes, she could handle a few days of passion. She'd slept with Daniel for four months without falling in love.

Carter's different, her conscience prodded.

She couldn't—*wouldn't*—fall in love with him again, but perhaps they could find pleasure in each other here in Atlanta away from prying eyes. The relationship would have to end once they returned home and she had the pictures in her possession. Anything more would be risky and ill-advised.

Phoebe reached for his belt buckle. Carter sucked a breath through clenched teeth and pulled her hands away. He peeled off his shirt and tossed it on a chair and then plucked at her dress. "How do I get this thing off?"

Ignoring the warning bells clanging in her head, Phoebe

grasped the hem of her dress. Carter helped her pull it over her head and then it landed on top of his shirt. She reached for him again, but he caught her hands and held them out by her sides.

His gaze poured over her like liquid flame. "You're beautiful."

She wasn't. But she wouldn't argue. Not now. "You make me feel that way."

He traced a finger along the lace edge of her white bra, down the center of her abdomen and along the waistband of her briefs. Granny panties. Phoebe's insides curled in embarrassment. She never wore sexy lingerie. What was the point when she was the only one who saw it? She found it much more practical to choose items that wouldn't leave telling lines beneath her clothing.

Dimples appeared in Carter's cheeks. "What are you hiding, Phoebe?"

The combination of his boyish grin and passion-filled eyes swept her mind of coherent thought. He knelt and kissed her tummy above the elastic. His fingers hooked behind the fabric and lowered it an inch, uncovering her navel. "Ah, this."

He delved his tongue into the shadowy indention. Heat radiated from her midsection. Phoebe gasped and staggered back against the table. She clutched the edge for support. Carter inched her panties down, kissing, tasting what he uncovered. He nuzzled her dark curls and steamed her with his breath. She bit her lip and struggled to inhale.

He sampled her skin from hipbone to hipbone, drawing erotic patterns with his tongue, and then he whisked the panties down her legs and urged her to step out of the satiny fabric.

Beginning at her ankles, Carter worked his way back up her legs, drawing circles with his thumbs until he returned to her curls. A needy sound slipped from Phoebe's lips when he parted her folds, found her moisture and spread it over her core. Her legs quivered. Her blood hummed in anticipation as his gaze locked with hers. He slowly lowered his head to taste her. Déjà vu.

At the first stroke of his tongue her eyes slammed shut on a wave of desire so strong it took all her willpower to remain standing. Had it not been for the table propping her up she would have sunk to the carpeted floor. The pleasure rose too swiftly. Phoebe wanted to plead for Carter to slow down, but she couldn't find her voice. She tangled her fingers in his hair and tried to ease him away.

He must have misunderstood her incoherent plea, because he nudged her legs farther apart and filled her with his fingers, which only made her ascend faster. Each stroke of his hand, of his mouth, brought her closer to the edge of control. And then it happened. Her muscles clenched and she cried out as the dam broke and pleasure rushed over her in waves.

Carter's hair brushed her stomach as he blazed an upward path with his lips, pausing only to release and remove her bra. He pulled one nipple into his hot mouth and cradled the other in his hand and tension began anew.

Phoebe's legs trembled. Near collapse, she tugged at Carter's arms until he rose to stand in front of her.

"Take me to bed, Carter."

Carter looked into Phoebe's passion-glazed eyes and his gut twisted. Something wasn't right. He wasn't supposed to feel this much or want her this badly. He ached to be inside her, but he didn't want to *need* her. Cuddling in bed would only worsen the situation.

"Who needs a bed?" He licked Phoebe's taste from his lips. Her flushed skin, kiss-swollen mouth and the red shoes she still wore sent his temperature into the stratosphere. He outlined her rounder curves with his hands, appreciating the difference between the girl he'd known and the woman in front of him. God, he'd love to photograph her exactly like this with hunger in her eyes and candlelight flickering on her pale skin.

He lifted Phoebe onto the table, stepped between her knees and smothered her surprised squeak with his mouth. Her breasts prodded his chest like tasers, electrifying him, weakening him. He cupped and caressed her until she arched her back and made a purring sound deep in her throat.

Had her skin always been this silky? Impossible. But she tasted the same. Smelled the same.

She loosened his belt and his pants. The touch of her hand against him as she worked his zipper threatened his control. When she hooked her fingers beneath the waistband of his boxers and brushed the backs of her knuckles against his erection he nearly lost it. She'd pushed him too close to the edge.

"Wait." He dug in his pocket and withdrew the condoms he'd kept there since launching Operation Seduction—not one for wishful thinking or even two for confidence, but three for absolute certainty this mission would succeed. He dropped the packets on the table.

Seconds later she shoved his pants and underwear to his ankles. Phoebe wrapped her fingers around him and stroked him from base to tip. She captured the drop of liquid and proceeded to torture the hell out of him by spreading it around the top of his shaft with her thumb. Hunger consumed him in a white-hot flash. He kicked his shoes and pants aside and reached for protection.

Seconds later Phoebe guided him home.

Not home, dammit.

He gritted his teeth and tried to concentrate on his plan as her slick heat surrounded him. Her gasps and the way she wound her arms around his neck and molded her breasts to his chest put the bellows to the fire licking at the base of his spine. He withdrew and thrust deep. Again. Again.

The rattle of glasses on the table penetrated his lust-filled brain. He forced open his eyes and noted the rocking candlesticks and the wobbling dinnerware. Hell, they were going to burn the hotel down. Cupping Phoebe's bottom, he lifted her and strode five steps to the sofa. He lowered her to the cushions without breaking the band of her legs around his waist and followed her down.

Her lips seared his shoulder and her nails scored his back, igniting an unbearable fire. She arched to meet each thrust, each kiss. Carter struggled to remember his agenda.

Make her beg.

Hell, he was the one who wanted to beg. Beg her to make this last all night, all week. Beg her to keep touching him, squeezing him. With difficulty, he slowed his pace and pushed himself up on straightened arms. He bowed his back to take the tight bud of her nipple into his mouth, shifted to circle her hot spot with his thumb, and fought to hold on to the ragged edge of reason. He trembled with the effort.

He dragged out her response, bringing her to the brink and backing off repeatedly until she thrashed beneath him. He struggled to hold on, but he was losing the battle. He couldn't take much more and was ready to concede defeat when she caught his face in her hands and looked directly into his eyes.

"Carter, please. *Please.*"

Something clicked as their gazes locked. He shoved the vulnerable feeling aside and groaned in triumph at her whispered words of surrender. He stroked her, pounded into her and pushed her over the edge. She cried out his name and her internal muscles contracted around him as she came. He gave up the fight and let his pleasure implode.

His arms shook in the aftermath and he couldn't remain upright. Gasping for air, he dropped to his elbows. Her arms curled around his waist. Her legs tangled with his and her breath steamed his sweat-dampened shoulder. Their slick torsos melded and the scent of their passion filled his nostrils.

She'd decimated him.

What shook him the most as his pulse slowed and his thoughts cleared was the critical error he'd committed. The moment he'd looked into Phoebe's eyes his target had been compromised and the mission had become personal. Too personal. What in the hell had happened here? Sex with Phoebe wasn't supposed to be better than before.

Time for damage control.

His lids grew heavy and he wanted nothing more than to tuck Phoebe into his shoulder and sleep with her in his arms, but because he wanted to hold her so badly that was the last thing he'd permit. Before he could release her, the featherlight glide of her fingertips along his spine sent an adrenaline surge through his veins.

His pulse, which had been slowing, picked up pace. The night wasn't over and he wasn't done with Phoebe yet. Nuzzling her temple, he whispered in her ear, "Your shower or mine?"

Seven

Cold sheets. An empty bed. Not what Phoebe had expected to awaken to this morning.

She lay in bed listening for sounds of Carter moving around in another part of the suite, but only silence greeted her. The surface of the pillow beside her was smooth and undisturbed. Carter hadn't shared her bed last night. The last thing she remembered was being warm and very satisfied in his lap in the chair across the room. He must have tucked her in after she'd fallen asleep.

The sheets dragged against her bare skin as she rolled over to look at the clock: 8:00 a.m. Carter had probably left for the work site already. She flopped back on her pillow feeling a little less excited about the day ahead than she had sixty seconds ago.

What had she expected? Cuddling? Breakfast in bed? She and Carter had never had the opportunity to spend an entire night in each other's arms. Why should that change now? Their first affair had been a series of stolen moments, and the current relationship would be more of the same. Angry with herself for her ridiculous expectations, she tossed back the covers and rose from the bed.

A short-term affair was exactly what she wanted. Wasn't it? So why did it feel so wrong? She *didn't* want more and couldn't have more, because she couldn't risk freeing the selfish urges inside her again. The last time she'd almost repeated her mother's mistakes and forfeited her family. Phoebe would never cause her grandfather the kind of pain her parents' desertion had caused her.

The hotel robe lay on the floor where Carter had dropped it last night when he'd peeled it from her body after their shared shower. The memory of hot, slippery sex in the steamy shower generated a rush of heat. Phoebe snatched up the robe and shrugged it on. The still damp fabric chilled her flushed skin.

After a quick walk through the suite to confirm that she was indeed alone, she showered while the mini-coffeepot dripped its eye-opening brew. Soaping her skin with her soft, manicured hands didn't feel nearly as good as Carter's slightly rough palms had last night. Phoebe paused beneath the shower spray. Everything about last night had been different.

Carter wasn't the eager but hesitant lover she remembered. Like a much-practiced master of the game, he'd played her by taking command of her body and delaying her satisfaction each time they'd made love until she'd begged him to take her over the edge. Certainly he'd found physical release, but he hadn't lost control the way he used to. He'd held something back. And he hadn't embraced her afterward. Twelve years ago they'd cuddled after making love until lack of time or a knock at the door had interrupted.

Inhaling an unsteady breath, she sagged against the cold

tile with a heavy heart. He was using her. Why did the knowledge settle heavily on her chest? This wasn't love. It was sex—*just sex*—and she was using him, too. Wasn't she? Hadn't she insisted on a three-day limit?

Like the familiar rides at the amusement park, an affair with Carter was something she could handle as long as she watched where she was going and stayed focused on the short-term nature of the thrill. This joyride into passion would end in roughly sixty hours. Sunday night, Carter would return the pictures and negatives and say goodbye.

She completed her shower and dressed, booted up her computer and tried to lose herself in researching quotes for her grandfather's speeches as she sipped coffee, but even Churchill's great orations couldn't keep her mind from straying.

If she only had two and a half days left with Carter, then she wanted to make the most of them. But how? She could plan a speech to wow an audience, but she had no experience planning an affair. If only she'd listened to the gossip in the break room at work...

At ten o'clock her cell phone vibrated beside her laptop on the desk. The Caller ID flashed Granddad. Phoebe hesitated, her hand hovering over the phone. She'd only lied to her grandfather once in her life—the day she'd lied about Carter being only a classmate. If she answered the phone she feared she'd have to fib again.

The phone buzzed once more. Duty won. She answered. "Hello, Granddad. How is the weather on the island? Are you playing golf from dawn to dusk?"

"I didn't call to talk about the weather. Daniel tells me you're on vacation. *With someone.* I was unaware that you were dating."

Phoebe's heart stalled. So much for hoping Daniel would keep quiet. It hadn't taken him long to go squealing to his boss. "I'm not dating anyone. I ran into an old friend and we're catching up."

"A man."

Phoebe sighed and silently cursed Daniel. "Yes."

"Anyone I know?"

"I don't think so. How's the campaign plan going?"

"I didn't call to discuss the campaign, either. It's you I'm worried about. Daniel says—"

"Daniel talks too much, and I hope you realize that not everything he tells you is true. Don't worry about me. I'm fine."

"Where are you?"

"Granddad—"

"Phoebe, you're all I have left. Don't I at least have the right to know where you are in case of an emergency?"

The guilt knife twisted beneath her ribs. She closed her eyes and sighed. "Atlanta. I'll be home Sunday evening."

"I'll cut this trip short. We're not doing anything here that can't be done in the office. Meet me back at the—"

"No." She tried to swallow her panic. "Stay and finish what you've started. You'd be interrupted by a million trivial things in the office. That's why you went to the island in the first place."

"You could join us."

She heard concern in his voice. "And interfere with your cigar smoking and golf? I don't think so."

Silence stretched between them. "Phoebe, your mother—"

He always brought up her mother when he thought she was stepping out of line. "We've been over this before. I'm not my mother. You can count on me to stand by you."

Another pause made Phoebe's stomach churn.

"No. You're much more sensible than Gracie, God rest her soul. This isn't someone special? Someone you'll be bringing home?"

"No, Granddad, he's no one special. I won't be bringing him home to meet you."

"Then I'll see you in three weeks unless you need me sooner. I love you, sweet pea."

"I love you, too." She disconnected. The heaviness returned to her chest. Carter had once been the most special man in her life, but now he could be nothing more than an interlude. Her grandfather came first.

A sound behind her made her turn. Carter stood in the open door of her room. Phoebe's stomach fell. How much had he heard?

No one special. An acid taste filled Carter's mouth.

Phoebe bit her lip and eyed him guiltily. "I thought you were working."

"I was." But the memory of Phoebe sexy, sated and rumpled when he'd deposited her in bed during the early morning hours had played havoc with his concentration. He'd turned the job over to his project manager and like a damned fool rushed back to Phoebe only to hear he was *nothing special.*

He'd make her eat those words.

Sawyer's and Rick's warning echoed in Carter's ears. Was he in over his head? Was the mission too compromised to continue? Should he abort? No, dammit. His pride might be dented, but he wasn't a quitter. He'd finish what he started, and he could still achieve a successful outcome if he got his head back in the game. Someone needed to teach Phoebe Lancaster Drew how it felt to be used and discarded. There was no one better qualified for the mission than him.

He loosened his tie as he crossed the room. She wanted a sex toy? Fine. He'd oblige until he had his fill of her.

The sunlight streaming through the open curtains revealed

that she'd already put on her makeup and twisted her hair into that schoolmarmish knot. Too bad. He intended to mess her up.

She dampened her lips, set the cell phone down and smoothed her hands over her tailored slacks. "What did you have planned for us today?"

He tossed the tie and his jacket over the back of a chair and reached for the buttons on his cuffs. Determined to fight dirty if the mission required it, he rolled back his sleeves. "Tonight we're attending a photography exhibit at a local gallery. If you didn't pack a formal dress we need to purchase one this afternoon. While we're out shopping we can visit the High Museum of Art, but we're spending the rest of the morning in bed."

Phoebe blinked. Wariness mingled with desire in her hazel eyes. "I—I'd like to see the museum and the photography exhibit, and I brought a black dress that should be suitable."

He lifted his hand and tangled his fingers in her hair. "Good. Then we have more time for this."

Carter swallowed his anger, lowered his head and captured her lips. He poured every ounce of seductive skill he'd learned over the past twelve years into the kiss. After a moment of stiff surprise, Phoebe curved against him and sighed into his mouth. Her soft breasts and hard nipples prodded his chest, sending a shock wave of sensation over him and wreaking havoc with his planned seduction. Her fingers curled into his waist and then pressed the tops of his thighs before she kneaded his butt. He yanked his head back and sucked in a sharp breath through gritted teeth.

Dammit. Sex with Phoebe shouldn't be this good. He'd banked on his memories being exaggerated. They hadn't been. Each brush of her fingers, each sip from her lips, turned him back into a randy college boy who'd just discovered sex. His impatience to slide into her slick heat nearly overwhelmed him.

Soften. Seduce. Sayonara. He silently chanted his game

plan as he struggled to dam the rising tide of desire in his blood. *Leave her wanting more.*

He stepped back, sat in the desk chair and rested his ankle on the opposite knee to conceal his condition. "Take down your hair."

Phoebe licked her bottom lip. Hesitantly she raised her arms and released her tightly twisted hair. The strands fell over her shoulders. He held out his hand and she dropped the pins into his palm. He tossed them on the desk. "Undress for me."

Her expression turned uncertain. "Carter—"

He leaned back in the chair and folded his arms. "You never had a problem stripping for me in the past."

"No, but…"

"Undressing for me used to make you hot."

Her cheeks flushed. "Yes, it did."

"Get naked for me, Phoebe. I want to see every inch of your skin. And then I plan to touch you, to taste you."

Her breasts shuddered on a slow inhalation, but she reached for the button on her slacks. The audible sound of her zipper sliding down had the impact of a fingernail tracing over his erection. He barely suppressed a shiver. Her pants slid to the floor, revealing long, bare legs that he knew from last night in the shower were silky-smooth. She picked up the pants, folded them neatly and laid them on the desk. Twelve years ago she hadn't been as conscientious. He wanted her as out of control today.

"Now the blouse."

Her throat worked as she swallowed. She released the top buttons, revealing the rapidly fluttering pulse behind her collar. The blouse parted to reveal a white bra. He'd seen sexier lingerie, but none of the seductive bits of satin and lace affected him as strongly as the sight of Phoebe shrugging off the stiff blouse. She carefully placed it atop her slacks.

Carter jerked his chin, indicating she continue. He liked the contradiction between Phoebe's sedate undergarments and the way she'd gone wild in his arms last night. On the sofa. In the shower. In the chair where he now sat. His pulse drummed loudly in his ears.

She removed her bra, revealing the plump mounds of her breasts and the stiff dusky peaks. Carter swallowed the rush of moisture in his mouth. He'd buried his face in her soft flesh last night. He extended his arm and she put the bra in his hand. He lifted it to his nose and inhaled. Her perfume filled his senses as he dragged in a lungful of air. Need throbbed in his groin. "You smell edible."

Phoebe gasped, dug her thumbs beneath the waistband of her panties and quickly shimmied the silky fabric down her legs. Eagerness, that's what he wanted from her. He mashed his lips together to conceal a smug smile. The fact that he was just as eager to have her hot, wet and hungry was a complication he didn't need.

She straightened and paused as if asking, What next? Carter savored her from the top of her mussed head to the twitching toes of her bare feet. He lingered over her breasts, the indentation of her waist and the soft swell of her hips. Beautiful. And his for the weekend. He set his feet on the floor, spread his knees and pointed to a spot on the carpet between them. "Come here."

Phoebe moved forward. The fine tremor of her body surprised him. Nervousness mingled with arousal in her eyes. He compressed his lips and shifted his gaze to her breasts. *Don't get personal.* But the vulnerability in her eyes disturbed him.

He caught her hands in his and carried them to her breasts. With his fingers laced over the back of her hands, he caressed her, letting her feel the pebbled tips and satiny skin with her palms. Did it arouse her as much as it did him? Phoebe's eyes closed. A sigh slipped past her lips.

He removed his hands, but left hers cupping her flesh. "Show me how you like to be touched."

Phoebe's eyes widened. Her cheeks turned scarlet. "Carter—"

"You used to love for me to watch."

She shifted uncomfortably. "Only if I get to watch you, too."

An onslaught of memories set off a string of explosions in his bloodstream. So much for detachment. Against his better judgment, he ground his teeth and rose. With quick, jerky movements he ripped off his shirt, kicked off his shoes and shucked his pants and boxers. He couldn't hide his arousal.

"That's better." A smile curved Phoebe's lips as her gaze inspected every inch of him. He remembered that self-satisfied smile and the absolute no-holds-barred pleasure that had always followed.

Lack of oxygen made his head spin. He sucked in a forgotten breath and sank back into the cool vinyl chair, prepared to play the copycat game they'd once enjoyed. Ignoring the throb in his groin, he mirrored her movements, stroking his chest, circling his tight nipples when she caressed hers. Goose bumps rose on his skin. When Phoebe raked her short nails over her abdomen, he did the same over his own, carefully avoiding his hard-on. His muscles contracted involuntarily. His jaw muscles ached and his heart pounded.

Phoebe's gaze never drifted from his hands as her fingers skimmed her hips and thighs and then sifted through the dark curls between her legs to reveal the moisture glistening there. His thumb encountered the slickness of his own arousal.

The cadence of her breathing changed and a flush swept across her chest. He knew what that meant. She was close. So was he. Holy spit. His grip tightened.

"Phoebe—" He bit his tongue on the plea for her to wrap her smooth fingers around his shaft and finish the job he'd started. He sure as hell liked her touch better than his own. Closing his eyes, he let loose a litany of silent curses as his control slipped. He'd be damned if he'd come in his own hand.

The air in the room shifted and then Phoebe's silky hair brushed the top of his thigh with the impact of a lightning bolt. He jerked his eyelids open in time to see her kneel in front of him and bend her head. His entire body clenched in anticipation. Her soft shoulders nudged the insides of his thighs as she leaned forward to trace his swollen tip with her tongue.

A groan erupted from his chest. *Hold on. Hold on. Hold on.*

Her hand surrounded him and then her lips parted and she took him into her hot, wet mouth. He dug his fingers into her hair, wanting to stop her, wanting her to *never* stop.

She stroked him with exactly the right pressure, lingered for precisely the right length of time, only this time was better than any time before. Her touch seemed surer, her mouth slicker, hotter. He was a second away from detonation when she released him and stood.

Air rushed from his lungs on a groan. "Don't stop, Phoebe. Please don't stop."

Phoebe walked to the bed, yanked back the covers and scooted across the sheets. She leaned against the headboard and clutched her knees to her chest as if suddenly shy. What she probably didn't realize was he had a clear view of heaven between her ankles from where he sat at the foot of the bed.

"If you want more, Carter, come and get it."

His heart nearly knocked a hole through his chest. With two strokes he could finish this without her and leave her wanting more. He was supposed to have her pleading, but dammit, she'd made him beg.

And now she'd have to pay.

Don't quit now, Phoebe chided herself, but as much as she ached to have Carter deep inside her at the moment, the angry passion in his eyes almost made her want to run into the bath-room and lock the door.

He would not play her this time. Determined to break his iron control, she'd turned the tables on him and, judging from his abrupt movements as he snatched up his pants and re-trieved a condom, he didn't like it.

Payback would be hell—pleasurable hell, no doubt. Her heart leaped in expectation as he approached the bed. "Only one this time?"

A muscle beside his mouth ticked. "I have more."

"Good. We'll need them." She extended her hand.

His chest expanded as he inhaled and his eyes blazed. After a moment's deliberation he placed the condom in her hand. Phoebe shoved it under the pillow and knelt on the edge of the mattress.

Carter stood beside the bed, a rock-hard wall of muscled, hungry male. Phoebe knew all of his erogenous zones and in-tended to hit each of them today. She wanted him absolutely out of control—the way she'd been last night and again a few moments ago. He reached for her, but she captured his hands. Beginning with his right, she traced a pattern over his palm with her tongue and then suckled his finger into her mouth. His eyes closed and his forehead pleated as if he were in pain. She repeated the torture with his left hand.

Carter pulled free and again reached for her. She pushed his hands away. "Not yet."

He clenched his fists by his sides and watched her through narrowed eyes. As much as their earlier game had aroused her, she needed to touch him herself. She opened her hands over his broad chest, combed her fingers through the dark hair scattered over his pectorals and then traced the thin line to his thick arousal. The combination of his hot skin and the tickle of hair against her palms made her shiver. Leaning forward, she sampled his collarbones, the softer skin beneath his ears and the barbed-wire tattoo on his bicep. His tiny nipples beaded beneath her tongue. She loved touching Carter, savoring his scent and tasting his skin, and she reveled in his swiftly indrawn breaths and the heavy pounding of his heart beneath her cheek. Hers beat equally as fast, and her breasts and womb ached, but she'd prolong this until one of them—*preferably him*—cried uncle.

Carter's muscles rippled involuntarily beneath the drag of her nails and again under the caress of her lips and tongue. He grabbed her waist, pushed her back on the mattress and came down beside her. Phoebe quickly climbed on top of him and pinned his arms beside his head on the pillow. With his superior strength he could easily have broken free, but he didn't struggle. She leaned down and kissed him, slowly stroking her tongue over the seam of his lips and then against the slickness inside. The wiry curls on his chest teased her breasts, startling a gasp of pleasure from her. Heat built low in her abdomen. She lowered her hips, gliding her wetness along the hot, hard length of him. Again and again, she rocked over him until her own hunger almost peaked. Had she ever wanted him this badly? A moan slipped from her lips, mingling with one from his.

She wanted him inside her, needed him inside, but Carter still held on to his iron control, so she denied them both. She stroked his length and he pulsed in her hand. Her fingers explored lower, cupping him, fondling the satiny skin. He made a choked sound and fisted the sheets in his hands. Phoebe danced her fingers lightly down his thighs and back up again. His muscles went rigid as she approached his shaft, but she detoured, tangling her fingers in his nearly black curls instead.

A dark flush swept Carter's cheekbones and a corresponding wave of heat swept over Phoebe's skin. She teetered on the brink of orgasm. This was crazy. Why deny them both what they each needed for the sake of some stupid power game? She reached for the condom, but it had been years since she'd applied one and she fumbled. It took several attempts to smooth it over his length.

Carter sprang to life the moment she finished. Ironically, now that she'd given up on pushing him beyond his limits, she'd apparently done exactly that. In one second he had her flat on her back. In another he'd parted her legs and in the third he'd filled her completely. Phoebe gasped for breath at the sudden shocking, electrifying surge of his body into hers and held him close. His mouth slammed over hers, swallowing her cries of pleasure as he thrust swiftly and repeatedly. Within moments the most powerful release of her life rocked through her. She bowed off the bed, digging her heels into the mattress and her nails into Carter's buttocks.

"Damn you," he groaned against her cheek as he shuddered in her arms. "Damn you for making me want you again."

Phoebe sagged against the mattress and tried to catch her breath. Triumph faded into sadness as her body cooled. She might have made Carter want her, but he'd made her want him, too, and that path led to a fork in the road. She didn't need a public opinion poll to tell her that a dead end, a broken heart or both lay ahead. A no-win situation.

She'd made him beg, dammit. Carter stabbed a button on his laptop.

His hunger for Phoebe was so great that if housekeeping hadn't interrupted this morning then he and Phoebe never would have made it out of bed for lunch or the trip to the museum. They'd scrambled into their clothing and rushed out of the room just like old times. The heady scent of their lusty morning had clung to him throughout lunch and the museum tour. He couldn't say what he'd eaten or name a single piece of art he'd viewed at the museum. When they'd returned to the hotel he'd dragged Phoebe straight into the shower and lost himself inside her.

It had been one hell of a Friday and it wasn't over yet.

He concentrated on his laptop and tried to block out the sounds coming from the other room of Phoebe getting ready for the gallery opening. While she dried her hair and dressed he downloaded the pictures from his camera onto his computer and fought the urge to join her and mess her up again. He shot back his cuff and glared at his watch and swore in disgust. They'd made love an hour ago. How could he want her again already?

This morning's sex had reminded Carter of the one-upmanship games he and Phoebe used to play. In the past the determined glint in her eyes had meant certain defeat for him, but by the time he'd noticed the warning signs today he'd been too far gone to care. She'd penetrated his defenses. He considered his surrender and his current need signs of weakness, and he didn't tolerate weakness.

A temporary setback. Operation Seduction would proceed as planned. *Soften.* Check. *Seduce.* Check. Only sayonara remained between him and mission complete. Less than forty-eight hours to go. The knowledge filled him with a sense of urgency.

The last file transferred. He opened up the software program and clicked on the first picture—the one he'd taken the day Phoebe had walked back into his life. She'd been sitting at his kitchen table waiting while he'd retrieved their intimate pictures and unaware of him pausing on the opposite side of his den and pulling out his ever-present digital camera. The tension and sadness in her face made his chest muscles constrict. He closed the image.

The next shot displayed her in the foyer of Sam's restaurant. Wide-eyed, she stared at the sweeping marble staircase with a rapt expression that reminded him of the girl he'd once known. On the bike ride she'd looked as if she had the weight of the world on her shoulders. He clicked through more pictures, but paused when he came to the one of Phoebe belting out a song at the ball game. She looked happy and carefree with a Braves' cap tilted sideways on her head. That was the girl he remembered, the one he'd wanted to marry and spend the rest of his life with. But that girl had been an illusion.

Choose, Phoebe. Either tell your grandfather the truth or we're through. Her silence to his ultimatum had been all the answer he needed.

The day after he'd left her in Washington he'd decided that if he couldn't have the future he'd planned with Phoebe, he'd return to the only family he'd ever known—the Marine Corps. During college he and Sawyer had discussed enlisting and letting the military make computer-age secret agents of them. They'd made plans to start up a computer software company together when they got out. But once Carter had met Phoebe he'd discarded the idea. He'd never drag a wife or kids through the life he'd led.

He'd met his parents at the airport and instead of introducing them to their future daughter-in-law the way he'd planned, he'd driven straight to the enlistment office and asked his father to go inside with him. For the first time in Carter's life he'd seen pride in Vic Jones's eyes.

Sawyer and Rick had been surprised when Carter had told them what he'd done. Sawyer had promised to enlist the day after graduation, but then Sawyer's parents had been killed in a car accident on the way home from graduation dinner and Sawyer's younger brother had needed him. Carter had been on his own. His friends had kept their promise to stand by him, writing letters that kept him sane during his deployment and showing him a good time during furloughs.

Too bad Phoebe hadn't kept her promise to love him forever. Scratch that. He didn't need anyone else in his life who didn't think he measured up.

He moved on to the shots of Phoebe at the amusement park looking as happy as a kid with her mouth opened over a wad of cotton candy in one, glowing with anticipation in line for the roller coaster she'd ridden four times in another and grinning in triumph when she'd won a cheap souvenir mug at the ball toss in the last. He'd been trying to soften her up, and he'd ended up having fun. Not part of his plan.

Who or what had drummed the life out of Phoebe?

Not his problem. No sympathy. Phoebe had managed to screw up her life without his help. She'd have to fix it on her own.

Eight

The gallery opening was no different than any other gallery opening Phoebe had ever attended, and because she loved art she attended quite a few. But this time Carter stood by her side, handsomely clad in another designer suit, making it difficult for her to concentrate on the artwork. Her mind persisted on reliving a different kind of art. Specifically the way Carter had painted her body with his soap-slick hands earlier. He had a master's touch.

Mentally shaking herself free of the sensual image, Phoebe sipped her champagne, focused on the photography display in front of her and tried to ignore the distracting heat of Carter's palm on her waist. She narrowed her eyes and carefully considered the collage. Carter's were better.

"Your pictures belong here, Carter."

His teasing smile sent desire spiraling through her system. "You want our pictures hanging in an art gallery? Have you become an exhibitionist, Phoebe?"

Her skin chilled in horror at the thought of their private moments being so publicly displayed. Her grandfather would never forgive her. "No. I meant the pictures I saw at dinner with your neighbors were as good as the ones hanging on these walls. You've captured more emotion in your subjects' faces and your composition is as good, if not better."

Denial filled his eyes. He opened his mouth, but Phoebe held up her hand. "Don't argue. I know what I'm talking about. I may have majored in government at Georgetown, but I minored in art history."

Carter's face flushed with either pleasure or embarrassment before he turned back to the display.

"Let's get out of here," he murmured without looking at her.

"I thought you said you'd waited months for this exhibit to open."

He shot her a quick glance and towed her to the next photo. "I did. But right now I want to take you to bed and keep your legs wrapped around me until you collapse against my shoulder in exhaustion. The way you did this afternoon."

Dizzying need rushed through her veins. The shallow but rapid movement of Carter's chest filled her with a sense of feminine power—one she'd better not learn to like. She wet her lips and moved to the next display.

Stunned, Phoebe jerked to a halt in front of a large black-and-white profile of a nude woman lying on her back on a slab of white marble. The photographer had used backlighting to reveal the peaks and valleys of the subject's outline, making her look more like a landscape than a person. The model's features, cast in deep shadow, were almost unrecognizable.

She closed her gaping mouth. Carter had taken almost the exact same shot of her twelve years ago, but he'd draped her over a rounded boulder by University Lake on a moonless autumn night and set a couple of kerosene camping lanterns behind the rock for backlighting.

Instantly she recalled the cool air caressing her skin that night. She could almost hear the rustle of fabric as he'd shed his clothing and the crunch of leaves beneath his feet as he'd circled the rock to extinguish the lanterns. The memory of the scorching heat of Carter's mouth and hands on her skin as he'd made love to her beside the lake sent a rush of excitement sweeping through her. Phoebe exhaled slowly and tried to shake off the past and the accompanying arousal. It seemed like a lifetime ago.

She blinked and suddenly she was back in the noisy gallery. *Evaluate the picture without prejudice, Phoebe,* but she made the mistake of meeting Carter's gaze. Did he remember? Oh, yes, his astonished expression mirrored her own and passion burned in his blue eyes.

She cleared her tight throat and strived for professionalism. "Yours is better. This one is cold and depressing. Like death. Yours is warm and vibrant and full of life."

The way you'd been, her conscience prodded. The photograph on the wall in front of her and the one locked in her memory were a direct contrast between Phoebe now and Phoebe then. Sometimes she felt as cold as the lifeless woman on the slab.

A sudden impatience to see their photos overwhelmed her. "I want to see the pictures when we get back to the hotel. All of them."

"Whatever you say, sugar." The husky timbre of his voice sent a shiver of need down Phoebe's spine. His fingertips sketched a circle on her hip.

"Carter," a male voice called from behind him. Carter banked the need in his eyes, lowered his hand from her waist and faced the newcomer. A tall, slender man with wispy blond hair approached with his hands outstretched. "Glad you made it."

"I wouldn't miss it." The men shook hands and then Carter turned to Phoebe. "Phoebe, this is Bo Rivers, the gallery owner. Bo, Phoebe Lan—"

"Phoebe Drew," Phoebe interrupted quickly. She'd spotted several members of the press earlier. Over the years she'd become very good at identifying and avoiding them. It was unlikely her face would be recognized, but her name certainly would since she attended so many newsworthy events with her grandfather. "I was telling Carter that his photographs belong here."

Bo nodded. "I agree. When you convince him, let me know. He's been a generous sponsor, but I can't talk him into displaying his art, and believe me, honey, I've tried."

"You've seen Carter's work?" Phoebe asked, carefully modulating her voice to conceal her rising panic. *Which pictures?* That annoying nerve began twitching beneath her right eye, revealing her stress to anyone who knew her well enough to recognize the sign. Did anyone know her that well? No, probably not. Since her breakup with Carter she hadn't let anyone that close.

"Some. Usually he brings a piece or two in to ask me where he went wrong, and I always tell him the same. Nowhere. He's good. Too bad he insists on wasting his time with computers."

"The success of CyberSniper is what allows me to sponsor your shows, Bo," Carter replied.

"So it is." Bo sighed dramatically. "Well, if you ever change your mind about your pix, you know where to find me." Bo waved at someone across the room and excused himself.

Carter scowled at Phoebe. "Let's go, Ms. *Drew,* before someone recognizes you."

Phoebe frowned in confusion. What had happened to his teasing good mood and the smoldering wait-until-we-get-back-to-the-hotel promise in his eyes? "I'd like to see the rest of the exhibit."

"And risk being seen with me? What would the senator say?"

His sarcasm cut deep and then understanding clicked. "Carter, the place is crawling with press. I didn't want to draw attention to myself tonight because then the media would be diverted from the artist's work to politics and my grandfather's upcoming campaign. That would hardly be fair to the photographer. Didn't you say it was his debut?"

He didn't look convinced. She left him and walked to the next grouping. Carter followed, stopping directly behind her. "If I'm not your dirty secret, then why won't you tell your grandfather we're involved?"

Phoebe couldn't catch her breath. She guessed Carter wasn't referring only to their present involvement. Her secrecy had been a bone of contention in the past. She looked around at the milling crowd and then led him to the less populated back hall of the gallery by the fire exit.

"When my mother was seventeen she fell in love with a construction worker renovating the Lancaster estate. My grandfather forbade her to see her lover again because he said she was too young, and he threatened to get my father fired if he and my mother didn't end their association. Granddad tried to run Dad off, and he might have been successful if Mother hadn't become pregnant with me.

"I had just turned eighteen when we met, Carter. I didn't tell my grandfather we were engaged because I didn't want him to think history was repeating itself and try to run you off." She plucked at her evening purse. "I was afraid he'd succeed."

Anger tightened his features. "And you never thought to mention this to me?"

"No. I thought you'd be insulted that I believed you could be bribed to dump me."

"Damned right I would have been, but you should have warned me what I was up against, Phoebe."

In the end he hadn't needed to be bribed to break her heart. "You didn't wait around for my explanation or answer any of my calls. I would have explained that all we needed was time, time for my grandfather to understand that it wasn't infatuation, time for him to see that you were the right man for me, time for him to realize I wasn't repeating my mother's mistakes."

Carter wiped a hand over his jaw and swore. "Hell, you didn't even come to my graduation. I thought you considered me good enough to screw but not good enough to marry."

His voice was as rough as the freshly blasted granite in the rock quarry Phoebe had visited with her grandfather during a union strike. Her heart contracted. She had hurt him.

"You were wrong." She managed to squeeze the words out past the lump in her throat. "And I explained about the ambassador's visit. My grandfather was hosting the dinner. I had to be there. I'm sorry I missed your graduation."

What would have happened if they'd had this conversation twelve years ago? Would he have insisted she choose between him and her grandfather or would he have understood the temporary need for silence and secrecy?

Bo materialized beside them before Phoebe could find answers to her questions or figure out where this new knowledge would lead them.

"I brought someone to meet you. Louis, this is Carter Jones, a loyal supporter of the gallery, and his escort, Phoebe Drew. Louis is the artist whose work you're enjoying tonight."

Phoebe smiled at the newcomer. "I notice you've used the same model in every picture. She's lovely."

Louis's smile turned sad. "Yes, she was."

"Was?" Phoebe asked.

"I lost Sophie to breast cancer last year. We took most of these photos before she began treatment. Sometimes you never know what a treasure you have until it's gone. And then it's too late."

Intense pressure weighted Phoebe's shoulders. No, you never knew how much time you had left with the ones you loved. She'd lost her parents and her grandmother swiftly and unexpectedly. She glanced at the silent man beside her. She'd been granted a second chance with Carter. Did she dare take it? Without a doubt she still had unresolved feelings for him, but did she love him? Would he hurt her again?

Her head whirled with the knowledge that she could easily fall for him all over again. What if the agreed-upon three days wasn't enough? Could she and Carter have a healthy relationship or would anything long-term between them tempt her to do the unthinkable and selfishly turn her back on Granddad the way her mother had?

Phoebe was afraid to find out.

Truth or more political spin? The honesty in Phoebe's eyes stunned Carter.

How could he have been so wrong? Because until the Marine Corps had knocked it off him, he'd carried a chip on his shoulder about not being good enough. He'd never measured up for his father, and no matter which base they'd lived on Carter had always been the outsider, the new kid, the tall, skinny geek. He'd expected Phoebe to find him flawed, as well. Had he been waiting for her to dump him twelve years ago? Yes, he grudgingly admitted. He'd been preparing for the end the entire time he and Phoebe had been together, storing up memories via photographs and waiting for her to come to her senses and find someone better than a rootless military brat who'd never had a steady girlfriend before he'd met her.

Carter took a mental step back to reevaluate Operation Seduction. Phoebe's disclosure tonight peppered his plan with more holes than Swiss cheese. He'd wanted to teach her a lesson, but he was the one learning—learning that she hadn't been the only one to make mistakes. His lack of self-confidence back then had contributed to their breakup.

In two days he was supposed to hand over the pictures and negatives, let Phoebe erase their past and walk out of his life. He wasn't ready to let go. Not yet.

Would he ever be ready?

He needed to go someplace quiet where he could think. "Let's get out of here."

This time Phoebe didn't argue. Her fingers curled around his, igniting his skin. She hustled to keep up with him as he all but dragged her to the sidewalk to flag down a taxi. She looked beautiful tonight and classy as hell. He'd wanted to show her off. At his request she'd left her hair down. It flowed like a glossy dark waterfall over her shoulders. She'd painted her kiss-swollen lips deep red, but her light makeup hadn't completely camouflaged the love bite he'd left behind her right ear this afternoon. Her short, black cocktail dress skimmed her figure with enough detail to make his mouth water and her legs... He inhaled deeply. Phoebe had amazing legs he noted as he followed her into the back of the cab and stepped into the fragrant cloud of her perfume.

Carter gave the driver the name of the hotel and sat back against the seat. He'd set Phoebe up to take a fall, but somewhere between the bike ride, the roller coasters and tonight's revelation, her rare smiles had ambushed him and he was the one falling.

Forget Operation Seduction. The revenge plot now left a bitter taste in his mouth. How could he deliberately hurt Phoebe when she was already unhappy? It'd be like kicking a wounded animal. He had proof of Phoebe's unhappiness in the pictures he'd downloaded. A need to wipe the sorrow from her eyes swelled inside him. He didn't know how to complete the task, but he knew he couldn't give her up without making some effort to help her get her life straightened out.

He'd made a name for himself nationally as a troubleshooter. The Fix It Wizard, one of his clients called him. Could he apply the skills he used at work to Phoebe's misdirected life? Analyze. Strategize. Attack.

What was it Rick had said? Something about sleeping with a woman to get her out of your system would only embed her more deeply under your skin? He owed his buddy a case of steaks for being right. Too bad Carter hadn't been smart enough to heed the warning, because now he was in over his head.

He'd be damned if he'd say goodbye without at least attempting to make his relationship with Phoebe work. But his business and Sawyer and Rick, his adopted family, were in Chapel Hill, and Phoebe's life revolved around Capitol Hill and her grandfather. An impasse, but not an insurmountable one.

He was absolutely certain he could make Phoebe happy. All he had to do was to convince her to leave Washington, a job she didn't like and her grandfather behind.

Not even the most proficient political spinner could hide the truth. Phoebe found herself facing another crossroads, torn between the two men she cared most about.

She scrambled to consolidate the facts and to formulate a palatable option. Carter had thought *she* had betrayed *him* when all these years she'd believed that, just like her parents, he hadn't loved her enough to stay.

Where did they go from here?

Supremely conscious of Carter standing behind her, she laid the photographs on the hotel table like playing cards in a game of solitaire. Memories swamped her and, as if the pictures had been taken yesterday, she remembered the emotion and arousal of each scene.

The past two weeks had proven that she hadn't erased the selfish streak she'd inherited from her mother. She'd only suppressed it, and Carter seemed determined to resurrect it. She needed to put some distance between them, to remind herself how close she'd come to losing everything and everyone important to her the last time she'd fallen in love with Carter and thought of no one but herself. Loving Carter again meant abandoning her grandfather at the most important point in his career, risking his rejection and losing the only family she had left.

She looked up into Carter's watchful eyes. "Give me the negatives and I'll get out of your hair so you can work."

He shook his head. "The negatives aren't here, and if you don't stay through Sunday then our deal is off."

A no-win situation. Carter's life and company were in North Carolina near his friends. He wouldn't move. She spent most of the year in D.C. She couldn't support her grandfather and have a serious relationship with Carter simultaneously. The past had taught her that long-distance love affairs didn't work.

"Carter—"

"No negotiation, Phoebe."

She closed her eyes briefly and searched for calm, for a solution, but found neither.

"You looked happier then," he said over her shoulder.

She opened her eyes and reexamined the images on the table. "I was surrounded by people I loved. My grandparents. *You.*"

He stepped behind her chair and bent over her, bracing his arms on the table on either side of her and caging her in place. Heat radiated off of his body, tempting her to lean back against his strength. "Which is your favorite? This one is mine."

He pointed to one square and instantly Phoebe relived the thrill of their first naughty, forbidden photo session and the feel of his body pressed intimately against hers while she waited impatiently for the camera's timer to go off. They'd made wild love afterward on the floor of the dorm room.

Blinking away the sensual haze, she evaluated the photograph he'd indicated. She and Carter were nude and facing the camera. He stood behind her with his arms wrapped around her. His left forearm covered her breasts and his big right hand completely hid the dark curls between her legs. His lips pressed the side of her neck, and her tumbled chestnut hair draped the opposite shoulder. Passion suffused her features and turned her hazel eyes a deep green.

Phoebe swallowed hard and took a slow breath. "What now?"

"That's up to you."

She stiffened. "What do you mean, 'up to me'?"

Carter knelt beside her chair and took her hands in his. Phoebe tensed at his somber expression. "I'm falling in love with you again, Phoebe, and while I'm not asking you to marry me yet, whatever was between us twelve years ago is still there. We owe it to ourselves to give it a shot."

He was falling in love with her. Her pulse raced and she couldn't catch her breath. She yearned to race headlong wherever this relationship led, but knew all too well the costs of such a decision. "I have feelings for you, too, Carter, but I don't know how we can make it work."

He rose, dragging her out of the chair and looping his arms around her waist. His hips pressed hers. "First, you have to decide that you're willing to try and then make your mind up what your future holds. Me or a job you don't like."

Phoebe gasped. Carter couldn't possibly know he'd just voiced her worst fear. "You're asking me to choose between you and my grandfather."

"I'm asking you to get off a dead-end road and straighten out your life. You're unhappy, Phoebe."

She fisted her hands against his chest. "My grandfather is

counting on me. I promised my grandmother I'd be there for him as long as he needed me and, right now, he needs me."

"You've given him the past twelve years. How much more time are you going to waste catering to him?"

"I don't consider it a waste of time."

"Then we have a problem."

She pulled away and hugged herself. "You don't understand. I owe him."

"For what?"

Shame heated her skin, but she had to make Carter understand the enormity of her debt. "For taking me in when my parents abandoned me."

"Your parents were killed. He's your next of kin. What else would you expect him to do?"

She'd never told him the entire story because she hated admitting that she'd inherited some of her mother's undesirable traits. "Yes, but my grandparents took over my care long before then."

Phoebe walked toward the window. The lights of Atlanta glistened beyond the glass wall, and she wished she were down there instead of up here having this difficult conversation. "My mother had a bad habit of doing whatever she pleased regardless of the consequences. She eloped with my father against her parents' wishes. Shortly after the wedding my father lost his job and his apartment. Because my mother was pregnant with me, my grandmother offered to let them temporarily move into my mother's old room.

"According to my grandmother, it wasn't a peaceful co-existence. My father made no attempt to get another job. He preferred to live off my mother's trust fund, which she'd inherited upon her marriage. And my mother and grandfather argued constantly because my mother lacked ambition. She wouldn't go back to school or get a job. All she wanted to do was to party and travel. I suspect alcohol and drugs might have been involved, but my grandmother wouldn't say. Mom left me in my grandmother's care most of the time. Granddad often threatened to throw Mom out if she didn't straighten up."

Phoebe hugged herself against the chill pervading her limbs. "The arguments used to terrify me. I didn't want to move away from my grandparents. I felt safe and secure with them. When I was seven, one of their screaming matches woke me. I crept out of my room and listened from the top of the stairs. My grandfather called my mother a selfish prima donna who never thought of anyone but herself. He ordered her to leave and not come back until she'd grown up. My mother screamed she'd never come back if growing up meant being a pretentious old windbag like him.

"My parents left that night and never returned. Their selfishness destroyed my family."

Carter pulled her into his arms and pressed her head against his chest. His lips brushed her brow. "Your parents' mistakes are not your fault."

Tears stung her eyes as she lifted her gaze to his. "You don't understand, Carter. After everything my grandfather has done for me I can't let him believe I'm just as selfish as my mother."

Nine

The vibrating cell phone roused Phoebe from her internal debate. She blinked and looked at the blank screen on the neglected computer in front of her. So much for working Saturday morning while Carter was away. She'd accomplished absolutely nothing.

She reached for her phone and glanced at the Caller ID. Her mouth dried. "Hi, Granddad, have you improved your golf score?"

"I want to meet him," he said without preamble.

Phoebe's heart missed a beat. "Who?"

She knew who.

"I don't believe he's not special. There has to be something about him to make you run off to Atlanta. You have never been reckless or irresponsible in your life. Why him? Why now?" He delivered his monologue with the power and resonance that riveted the jaded members of the senate and swayed voters. She could picture him punctuating the last two questions with a fist pounding on a podium or his desk.

She had been reckless and irresponsible before, only Granddad didn't know that, and she wasn't sure how to break it to him. Would he think less of her? Would he be horrified by her actions? Would he be able to forgive her? "It's a little premature for bringing him home to meet the family."

"Phoebe, your mother chose unwisely. I'd like to make sure you're not making the same mistake."

Guilt constricted her ribs. "Granddad, I'm thirty years old—too old for you to be cleaning up my mistakes."

"Your grandmother would want me to meet him, to make sure he has your best interests at heart."

She sighed. Whenever dragging her mother into an argument didn't work, her grandfather pulled out heavier weaponry—her grandmother. An image of Naomi Lancaster's censuring face instantly flooded her mind. Phoebe had lost count of the times a simple, "Your grandmother would be disappointed" had jerked her back in line. Not that her grandmother hadn't loved her, but Naomi Lancaster had been a firm disciplinarian who'd tolerated no nonsense.

Phoebe acknowledged that her refusal to be completely truthful about the depth of her feelings for Carter the last time she'd introduced the two men had contributed to the end of the relationship, but even after two hours of deliberations this morning, she couldn't see a way around this stalemate. The fact remained that she'd have to choose one man or the other, and she wanted to postpone that painful decision for as long as possible because either way, she'd lose.

"Maybe in a few weeks if we're still seeing each other."

She suspected that wouldn't be the case.

Sunday evening Carter faced the fact that for the first time in three years he wasn't looking forward to returning home after a job out of town.

Would the real world pull Phoebe away?

As if she shared his unease, Phoebe had remained tense and silent during the drive from the airport to her grandfather's home in Raleigh. She suddenly jerked upright in the front seat of Carter's Mustang. "He's home."

"Who?"

"My grandfather. His car is in the driveway. He wasn't due home for weeks." Her voice was little more than a whisper.

Would she continue hiding their relationship? Carter considered demanding an introduction, but he and Phoebe were treading thin ice. Forcing her hand could mean losing her. The past two days had been something of an armed truce. They'd made love morning, noon and night, but avoided discussing the future during their trips to the theater Saturday night and the zoo this morning.

Patience, he told himself. *Show her the life she could have and she'll choose to leave the unhappiness behind.* But he wasn't as certain of success as he'd been before her revelation Friday night. Phoebe seemed convinced she had to pay for her mother's sins.

Carter pulled the car over by the curb on the tree-lined street and awaited instructions. Knotting her fingers, Phoebe cast him a desperate glance. She turned back to the sprawling Lancaster estate. He was used to giving orders. Sitting back and waiting for Phoebe to make up her mind was as uncomfortable as finding himself hunkered down over an anthill in the rainforest with the enemy surrounding him. He couldn't move or speak without attracting fire, but taking no action also led to pain.

"Let's go." She sounded resigned.

"Where?" He refused to let himself hope.

Her nod indicated the long, curving driveway. "Home."

Victory swelled in his chest. Carter put the car in motion,

but his nerves stretched tighter with each yard they covered. The series of cramped military married housing apartments in which he'd grown up could all fit together under the Lancaster roof with room to spare.

Carter loved graceful older homes and the sense of permanence that emanated from them. That's why he had allowed Rick to talk him into buying the house he now owned even though the place had needed a seemingly endless list of renovations. Phoebe had spent her childhood in this imposing structure. Had she been allowed to run in the halls, slide down the banister and dig in the yard the way Carter had always imagined normal—translation, nonmilitary—kids did? He'd always assumed kids with regular houses had it made. Looking at the manicured grounds encircling Lancaster estate he'd bet Phoebe's life hadn't been at all normal.

He parked beside a vintage Jaguar in the brick courtyard, got out and circled to open Phoebe's door. His knee ached the way it always did when he was tense. Phoebe hesitated before alighting as if gathering her courage. Carter reached into the trunk to extract her luggage and laptop briefcase. The front door clicked open as loudly as a pistol cocking beside his temple. His muscles clenched. Showdown.

He slowly turned to face the man firmly planted between Carter and Phoebe's future together. Wilton Lancaster stood framed in the entryway. The senator wasn't tall or broad, and yet he carried his average size with the bearing of a leader—one who commanded respect and would accept nothing less. Beside Carter, Phoebe looked as stiff and unsure as a new recruit during inspection. After a moment's hesitation she started forward, climbing each step with the precise pace of a casket-carrying honor guard. Would this be the funeral for their relationship?

Carter unlocked his muscles and followed. Phoebe stopped in front of her grandfather on the landing and pasted on what

Carter now referred to as her politician's smile. To a casual observer the curve of her lips looked genuine, but the smile didn't reach her eyes.

"Granddad, this is Carter Jones. Carter, my grandfather, Wilton Lancaster."

"I never forget a face," the senator said before Carter could reply. He subjected Carter to a thorough inspection. Was the man trying to intimidate him? Carter's officer training had taught him to never back down from a challenging glare. The senator would have to do better if he wanted to scare him off. Carter held his gaze.

"I imagine that's an asset in your career." Carter set down Phoebe's case, accepted the handshake. Firm, but not a bone-crushing test of strength.

"We've met."

"Yes, sir. Twelve years ago in D.C."

"Phoebe's classmate."

So the rumors of the senator's remarkable memory were true. Perhaps Lancaster wasn't too old to run for president after all. "Yes, sir."

"You'll stay for dinner." An order, not an invitation.

Carter looked at Phoebe's pale face, at the nerve twitching beneath her eye. He'd figured out that nerve only twitched when she was stressed and uneasy. Her pulse fluttered frantically at the base of her neck, confirming his deduction. "Phoebe?"

She nervously wet her lips. "Yes, please stay for dinner."

"Then thank you, sir. I accept."

"Inside." Lancaster turned on his heel and led the way. Inside the foyer the senator turned to Phoebe. "Tell Mildred we have a dinner guest."

Phoebe hesitated, clearly uncertain about leaving Carter and her grandfather alone together. Carter smiled and mouthed,

Go ahead. With obvious reluctance, she left them. The senator stepped into a room to the left of the foyer. Carter set Phoebe's bags down at the base of the wide staircase and followed. The study with its deep green walls, rich cherry desk and floor-to-ceiling bookcases looked like something from one of his neighbor's decorating and renovating magazines.

"You took my granddaughter to Atlanta."

"Yes, sir."

Lancaster crossed the expensive-looking Oriental rug, poured two bourbons and handed one crystal glass to Carter without asking if he wanted it first. The senator circled behind the desk and took a seat. He didn't invite Carter to sit down in one of the leather guest chairs. "Why?"

Carter sipped his drink before responding. The aged liquor slid down his throat like nectar. The senator had good taste. "I had business in Atlanta and I didn't want to be away from Phoebe."

"What kind of business?"

Carter set his glass on the desk, extracted a business card from his wallet and passed it to the senator. The card identified him as CEO of CyberSniper. Seeing his name embossed on the ivory card still filled him with pride. The company was absolute proof that Carter Jones, computer geek, had made a success of himself. He suspected the senator would use the information on the card to run a background check. "Installing a software security program."

Phoebe rushed back in. Her gaze bounced from Carter to her grandfather and back as if she were expecting to find a gauntlet on the floor between them. Her cheeks were flushed as if she'd hurried. "Mildred would like for us to go on through to the dining room."

Lancaster led the way and sat at the head of the long rectangle with Phoebe to his right and Carter to his left. The table was loaded with crystal, china and silver. Carter made a mental note to thank Sam for teaching him about fancy place settings. The cook set the first course in front of them.

"Thank you, Mildred." Phoebe turned to her grandfather. "How was your trip?"

Her grandfather scowled. "It rained and Daniel became ill and left early Friday morning. No point in staying if we can't get anything done." He stabbed at the salad. "Rabbit food. I want a steak."

"The doctor said—" Phoebe started.

"I know what he said." The senator set down his fork and shoved the plate aside. He fixed his eyes—the same green-gold hazel as Phoebe's, Carter noticed—on Carter. "I'm sure you're aware that Phoebe is my speech writer and my hostess. When I'm elected she will continue those duties. My constituents have already stated their desire for her to take over my senate seat after we leave the White House."

Phoebe made a choking sound and reached for her water glass, but she didn't object to the senator's announcement.

The senator expected Phoebe to run for office? "Have you asked Phoebe what she wants?"

Lancaster fixed him with a formidable stare. "The Lancaster family has served this country for more than a century. Phoebe will do her duty."

Carter could see desperation in Phoebe's eyes. "That's years away, Granddad. Let's get through this campaign first."

Carter gritted his teeth. His future with Phoebe depended on her speaking up for herself.

The senator's fist hit the table, making the crystal and silver rattle. "I won't have my granddaughter exposed to unsavory and damaging gossip, and any man involved with her also has to be above reproach."

"I have Phoebe's best interest at heart, sir. Do you?"

The darkening of the senator's skin was the only sign of anger. His expression didn't change. "I know my granddaughter better than you, boy, and I know what's best for her."

Boy. That reminded Carter of the arguments with his father and the need to prove himself rose swiftly within him, but he bit his tongue. This wasn't his battle. It was Phoebe's. He hoped she had the guts to fight it. If not, their relationship would be the first casualty.

Eager to see the end of an absolutely miserable evening, Phoebe walked Carter to his car.

She loved him.

Part of her wanted to hide in her room to digest the feelings rumbling around inside her. The selfish part of her wished she could climb into his car and leave with him, but neither was a viable option. She couldn't hide her head in the sand or run away. She had to go back inside and face her grandfather.

"You have to tell him you're unhappy, Phoebe."

Mildred's divine soufflé sat like an anchor in Phoebe's stomach. "I can't disappoint him right now. He needs to focus on the campaign."

"So what are you going to do? Hope he's forced into retirement by losing the election? If that happens, he expects you to run for senate in two years. You have to take control of your life, before it passes you by."

Her head ached from the constant verbal sparring over dinner. She didn't want to argue with Carter. Her grandfather wouldn't lose the election. Even this early he was the heavily favored candidate.

"I'll talk to him. But in my own time." She didn't want to have to choose because choosing meant losing. There had to be another way. Or was having it all as impossible as it seemed?

Had she ever met a man who could hold his own against the senate's most accomplished debater? No. Carter had been polite and respectful of her grandfather, but he hadn't been intimidated or backed down when asked to defend his views the way Daniel or any of the other men she'd dated did.

Had she ever met a man who made her want to be selfish and resurrect those old dreams of a home, family and children? Not until Carter.

And no matter how slyly her grandfather had pried, Carter hadn't let one single detail of their past or their present arrangement slip. He'd protected her, and he was trying to help her now. She sighed and tried to memorize his face. She had to make him understand the cost for letting her grandfather down, but tonight she wasn't up to the task. Maybe tomorrow she would have regained her equilibrium and her skill with words.

Carter pulled his keys from his pocket, took one off the ring and pressed it into her palm. His fingers closed over hers. "Here's a key to my house. Meet me there tomorrow evening. I should be able to get out of the office by five. If you get there before I do, go in and make yourself comfortable." He winked. "I would love to find you waiting in my bed."

Her breath hitched. The metal key had absorbed his body heat. She clutched its warmth. "I'll try, but I can't promise I can get away."

"You're the one who elected to pick up the negatives tomorrow instead of fighting traffic tonight. Remember?"

The negatives. How could she have forgotten the negatives? "Yes."

Carter extracted a business card from his pocket and wrote a series of numbers on the back. "This is the alarm code. Type it in as soon as you enter the house. Until tomorrow."

He angled her so that his back was between her and the house, pulled her close and lowered his head. His lips captured hers softly and then with increasing hunger. One palm cradled her face and then slid into her hair to cup her nape. The other banded around her waist.

Phoebe soaked up the heat of his body and the passion of his kiss. His touch made her feel alive and full of hope. How could she live without this, without him? She couldn't. Politics was all about compromise, and somehow, some way, she would find a compromise between making her grandfather happy and making a future with Carter. If only she knew how.

The phone rang Monday morning at five, jarring Phoebe from her troubled dreams. It rang again and again each time she started to drift back off to sleep. The senator never received calls this early in the morning unless there had been a crisis or a major news break. Either meant work for her. She'd need to be briefed so she could compose his comments on the subject.

Sluggish from a late night followed by tossing and turning, Phoebe dragged herself through her morning ritual. Sometime in the wee hours she'd come to the conclusion that Carter was right. She had to talk to her grandfather today and explain her feelings about Carter and about the job, but she hadn't figured out what she would say or how her grandfather would react. The wastebasket beside her bed overflowed with discarded attempts.

She followed the aroma of fresh-brewed coffee to the kitchen. Mildred turned as soon as Phoebe entered. "The senator wants to see you right away."

"Before breakfast?" She usually ate with the housekeeper. Phoebe poured herself a cup of coffee and sipped, hoping the black brew would clear the haze from her brain. "What happened? Has war broken out? Has the Speaker of the House resigned?"

Mildred's concerned expression turned Phoebe's stomach into a snarl of worry. "Go see your grandfather, child."

The coffee burned her stomach. Phoebe set her mug down. "Is something wrong?"

"Go."

Having worked for the Lancasters for more than twenty years, Mildred knew as much about world affairs as Phoebe. They'd often discussed troubling issues over the morning paper. That Mildred wouldn't chat now wasn't a good omen.

Phoebe found her grandfather in his study with the seven newspapers to which he subscribed piled in front of him. The fax machine whirred out pages in the corner. His computer was on and the armoire was open to the television streaming CNN. He had a phone pressed to his ear. From where she stood it looked like morning as usual in the Lancaster household, except for the strain on her grandfather's face, which aged him ten years.

What in the world had happened? Adrenaline pumped through Phoebe's veins in anticipation of tackling the latest issue. She was good at her job, and she knew whatever the issue she could handle it.

As soon as he spotted her, he ended his call. His solemn gaze nailed her to the Oriental rug. Phoebe hadn't seen that expression since he'd told her that her mother and father weren't coming home. Her mouth dried. "What's wrong?"

He lifted a paper from the top of the stack and passed it to her. She glanced at the top half of the page, skimmed the headlines and then unfolded the paper. The picture of her sitting naked in Carter's lap was the center story of the political page of a national paper.

Senate Staffer's Scandalous Secret.

Shock sent her reeling. She sank bonelessly into a chair. Oh, my God. Who? How? Why? Questions tumbled around in her head. To damage her grandfather's campaign of course. Shame burned her face and she wanted to throw up. The article speculated that if the senator couldn't control his own granddaughter how could he be trusted to run the country. The reporter even rehashed her mother's indiscretions.

Clenching her teeth against the nausea, Phoebe lifted her gaze to her grandfather's. Anger and disappointment mingled with hurt on his lined face.

This was the picture Carter had given her after their second date. She hadn't been able to destroy it, after all, and had hidden it in her nightstand upstairs. It was still there. She'd checked before going to bed last night. Carter must have made a duplicate. He said he had the capability. "I can explain."

"Is this what you were doing in Atlanta?"

"No." She inspected the picture more closely. The grainy black-and-white photo made it impossible to tell her age in the photo. "This is from…twelve years ago."

"Is that Jones?"

"Yes. He…" There was no point in keeping the secret now. "Carter and I were lovers during my freshman year of college."

He accepted the news with no show of emotion. "Who's the photographer and are there more pictures out there?"

"Carter took the picture with his camera set on a timer." Nervousness nearly strangled her. "And yes, there are more."

He exhaled. "I'm disappointed in you, Phoebe. I thought you'd been spared your mother's selfishness. Your grandmother would be appalled by your shameless behavior."

The verbal blows pummeled her. "I don't know how this got to the papers. Only Carter and I have access to the pictures."

"Then your lover betrayed you."

A sharp, stabbing pain in her chest made her flinch. She couldn't believe Carter would deliberately hurt her. Someone else must have found and leaked the picture. "He wouldn't."

"I've called a staff meeting for nine. We'll formulate a damage control plan and prepare a press release. You will explain this away as youthful folly, but that's unlikely to be enough to excuse your actions."

"I loved him."

"That's irrelevant. The pictures are pornographic."

She stifled the urge to squirm under his hard stare. Her hands trembled so badly the newspaper rustled like falling leaves. "They're not. They're erotic, yes, but you'd see more if I were wearing a swimsuit."

"Voters will disagree. Phoebe, you understand this will damage the current campaign and certainly any future campaign you might launch." His voice was harsh and unforgiving.

Her world was crumbling. Fear quickened her breath and hurried her pulse. "Yes, sir. That's why I sought out Carter. I wanted to get the pictures back. I'm supposed to pick up the negatives tonight."

"Get them now."

"But the staff meeting—"

"You have created the problem, Phoebe. We will inform you of the solution. I expect your full cooperation."

"Yes, sir. I'll get the negatives."

But what was the point? The damage was done. Her skeletons had come out of her closet.

Ten

Phoebe couldn't believe Carter would betray her. So if not him, then who? Someone had to have stolen his copy of the picture. The fact that Carter had made copies without telling her buzzed in her conscience like an annoying mosquito.

Carter didn't answer his cell or home phone. In a panic, Phoebe hung up without leaving a message on either and dialed his office. The receptionist put her through to his assistant. "I urgently need to speak to Mr. Jones."

"I'm sorry. Mr. Jones is taking another call at the moment and can't be disturbed. May I take a message?"

What could she say without giving too much away? "Tell him Phoebe called and that I need to move our evening appointment forward. The sooner he can see me, the better. In fact, I'm headed to the agreed-upon location now. Would you have him call me the minute he gets this message?"

She recited her cell phone number, ended the call and

turned her car into Carter's neighborhood. Retrieving the negatives couldn't wait. She had to have them now. And then she had to destroy them.

Pain squeezed her heart. Viewing the pictures with maturity, hindsight and an art history degree, Phoebe saw the value of Carter's developing artistic abilities. Certainly, all of the poses were sexy, but none were vulgar. And she wasn't ashamed of them. But in the wrong hands they could cause her grandfather tremendous embarrassment.

Carter had kept the pictures safely hidden for years. Couldn't she do the same? She didn't want to shred them. They represented the happiest time in her life. But she needed to assure her grandfather that all of the photos and negatives were in her possession and no longer a threat… Unless whoever had released this one had copies of the others. The possibility made her stomach hurt.

Entering Carter's house without him made Phoebe uncomfortable. *He invited you. Get it done.* Using the key he'd given her, she let herself inside and then punched the security code into the alarm system. Surely the negatives would be in the same location as the photos? She forced herself to move toward the master bedroom and paused on the threshold, reluctant to invade his privacy and begin searching, but search she must. Where should she start? Phoebe took a bracing breath and scanned the room.

A king-size bed covered in a chocolate-brown microsuede duvet dominated the large rectangular room. The dark wood furniture had an old world feel as if Carter were trying to create a sense of permanence.

I would love to find you waiting in my bed, he'd said. She blinked away an image of the two of them tangled in the sheets.

A bookshelf in the corner held a row of leather-bound

photo albums like the one she'd seen at dinner. That seemed as good a place to start as any. She crossed the room and pulled out the first book. A gangly, dark-haired boy with a gap-toothed grin and huge blue eyes stared back at her. *Carter.* He couldn't have been more than seven or eight years old in the picture. Phoebe turned the pages more slowly. Was the stylish woman his mother? The unsmiling man had to be his father. He shared the same eyes, square jaw and height. As much as Phoebe wanted to linger, she didn't have time. She needed to get back with assurances that all was under control before her grandfather's meeting concluded.

She flipped through the second book, wishing she had time to linger over Carter's teen years. The next volume was the one she'd looked at with Lynn and Lily during dinner. Two books held photos of Carter and uniformed men, and the last book contained pictures of Carter and his neighbors. She hadn't found the negatives tucked inside of any of the books, and there were no bins or boxes on the shelves in which to hide them.

Frustrated, she rose and grimaced at her watch. She was running out of time. Standing in the center of the room, she looked for something, *anything,* in which he might store pictures and saw nothing, and she was reluctant to riffle through his drawers. Next she entered the vast and mostly empty walk-in closet, hoping to find a safe or chest. No luck. And the few boxes on the shelves above the designer suits held only shoes. She returned to the bedroom and checked behind the landscape for a wall safe like the one back home. Nothing.

Her cell phone buzzed. She checked the Caller ID and cringed. Daniel. Less than a week ago she'd been tempted to mention her pictures just to shut him up. Now he knew and she was sorry to have to share her private moments with him.

"Yes," she clipped.

"We have a strategy. You're needed here."

"I'm in Chapel Hill. It'll take me forty-five minutes to get there."

"We'll begin preparing the press release. You've really done it this time, Phoebe. He may not forgive you." He disconnected.

Phoebe pressed a hand over her frantically beating heart with Daniel's words ringing in her ears. She had to make this right to earn her grandfather's forgiveness.

She needed to leave Carter a note telling him about the newspaper and asking him to call her. She looked around for something to write on and saw nothing. The furniture surfaces were clear. Apparently, Carter was something of a neatnik— a trait they shared. But she remembered a pad of paper beside the microwave in Carter's kitchen when he'd set her on the counter to bandage her blisters.

Seconds later she'd reached the kitchen, but the polished counters were bare. Phoebe cursed—a rarity for her—but her patience and politeness were wearing thin. She yanked open the drawer beneath the phone, found a legal pad and pen and carried both to the table while she mentally composed her message. She flipped through the pages looking for a blank sheet.

The words on the last page stopped her in her tracks.

Operation Seduction

Objective: teach Phoebe how it feels to be used and dumped.

Strategy:

Soften.

Seduce.

Sayonara.

M.O.: Candlelit dinners. Bike ride. Museum. Ball game…

The blood drained from her head so quickly she thought she might faint. She clutched the table for support and slowly collapsed into a chair. Tears blurred her vision, but she didn't need to read the rest of Carter's list to know she'd been set up. *Used* in a personal vendetta.

Suddenly she felt dirty and stupid. While she'd been falling in love, Carter had been plotting her downfall with military precision. Hysteria rose in her throat. Phoebe gulped it down. On the drive over to Carter's she'd made a half dozen guesses on who could have leaked the photo. People who wanted to hurt her or her grandfather. People who might want to split her and Carter up. Carter hadn't been on her list of suspects.

But now Phoebe knew without a doubt that no one had stolen the picture. Carter had turned it over to the paper, and he'd done it deliberately to hurt her. She'd often seen a hard glint in his eyes. Understanding dawned. He'd purposely given her hope and then he'd ruthlessly slapped it away.

Anger flared, quickly consuming her pain and humiliation. She picked up the black marker and scratched *"You bastard"* over top of his list. Phoebe rose on shaking legs, dug his house key out of her purse and slammed it down on the telling document.

Her parents had used her to keep her grandparents from throwing them out.

Daniel had used her to get to her grandfather.

Carter had used her for revenge.

Phoebe squared her shoulders and took a sobering breath. She was sick and tired of being a pawn in other people's games. That ended now.

Her cell phone rang. Phoebe checked the Caller ID. Carter Jones. She punched in the code to block his calls. She had nothing more to say to the man who'd broken her heart twice. She'd let her grandfather's lawyer do the talking.

* * *

You bastard. Carter spotted Phoebe's message the moment he stepped into the kitchen. He swore. No wonder she wasn't answering his calls.

How could she believe he'd betray her when he'd promised that he'd never use the pictures to hurt her? He wiped a hand over his face. Because she'd seen Operation Seduction in his own handwriting. What else was she to believe?

He'd walked away twelve years ago without stating his case and he'd lost Phoebe. Not this time. He'd find her. Explain. Make her understand. While he was at it, he needed to find out who'd leaked the picture. Had Phoebe? Was she using him to break her grandfather's choke chain? She'd always put her grandfather's needs first. This didn't seem like a choice she'd make.

The newspapers had been waiting on his desk when he'd arrived at work. Jes, his assistant, had wisely kept silent over his boss's sudden notoriety. Carter had spent the morning on the phone with clients who now doubted his credibility and needed assurances. He'd also had calls from Sawyer and Rick and several corps buddies offering their support.

He should have called Phoebe the minute he'd spotted the picture, but he hadn't known what to say. He'd wanted their relationship out in the open, but not this way.

Carter retrieved the negatives from the secret compartment in the back of his dresser and climbed into his car. Thirty minutes later he turned the Mustang into the Lancaster driveway and parked behind a number of other cars, including Phoebe's.

Mildred answered the door. Her scowl could frighten small children. "What do you want?"

"I need to see Phoebe."

"She's not in."

"That's her car in the driveway. Tell her I have the negatives."

Mildred shut the door in his face. Carter shoved a hand through his hair. Had he been dismissed or was she calling Phoebe? He'd have to find another entrance if the housekeeper refused to let him in, because he wasn't leaving without talking to Phoebe. He surveyed the front of the house, checking his options. The front door reopened to reveal the senator and another dark-suited man to his right.

"I want to talk to Phoebe," Carter restated.

"Phoebe doesn't want to see you, Mr. Jones. This is my attorney, Roger Kane. You can talk to him and hand over the negatives."

Carter silently swore. His muscles clenched. "No, sir. I'll give them to Phoebe or no one."

After a quiet word from his attorney, the senator grudgingly stepped aside for Carter to enter. Inside the foyer Carter noted the door to the study remained tightly closed, but the buzz of voices penetrated the heavy wood. Lancaster leveled his cold, hard gaze on Carter.

"Senator, I loved your granddaughter twelve years ago, and I love her now. I would never do anything to hurt Phoebe. I did not send the picture to the press."

A staring match ensued. Carter didn't back down. He wanted Phoebe's grandfather to see the truth in his eyes.

Finally the senator blinked. "If you are lying, Jones, you will regret it. I will personally—"

"Sir—" the attorney cautioned.

Lancaster nodded and pointed to the room behind Carter. "Wait in the living room. I'll get her."

Carter paced in front of the window in the formal white room. His business would survive the scandal. Would his relationship with Phoebe?

A sound at the door caught his attention. He turned and found Phoebe framed in the entry. She looked like hell. Red rimmed her eyes and her makeup couldn't disguise the pallor of her skin. Her tightly pinned-back hair only accentuated the strain in her features. The nerve twitched beneath her eye. He wanted to take her in his arms, but rammed his hands into his pockets instead. His embrace wouldn't be welcome.

"Say your piece and then leave." Pain filled her voice.

"Close the door."

She did as he asked, but didn't move any farther into the room. A good twenty feet of white carpet separated them.

"I told you I'd never use the pictures to hurt you."

She made a sound of disbelief. "You don't think giving one to the paper hurts me?"

Her lack of trust wounded him. "You immediately assumed I leaked the picture?"

"Not until I saw Operation Seduction."

Given the evidence, he'd probably find him guilty, too. He closed the distance between them. "I didn't leak the picture, Phoebe. Did you?"

Surprise widened her eyes. She backed up against the door. "Me? Why would I do such a thing?"

"Because you don't have the courage to tell your grandfather that you're unhappy and want out of Washington. Sullying your image will get you relieved of your duties."

Color flooded her pale cheeks. "Don't try to blame this on me. You leaked the picture because you wanted to force my hand. I chose my grandfather over you last time and you've held a grudge. You wanted to make me fall in love with you so I'd choose you and alienate my grandfather. And then you planned to walk away and have your revenge."

Her voice rose with each sentence until she was almost yelling at the end. She pressed her fingers over her lips.

Her accusation was too close to his original plan for comfort. He'd been an ass. "Phoebe, you're right. I did want to hurt you, but then I fell in love with you and I couldn't go through with the plan."

"You expect me to believe that? You took me to Atlanta with the sole intention of getting me into bed by softening me up with a Braves game and a trip to the amusement park. And fool that I am, I fell for it." The agony in her eyes cut him deeply. "I don't guess there's any point in asking for the negatives or the rest of the pictures. As you pointed out, scanners have made negatives obsolete."

He handed her the envelope containing the negatives. "I didn't copy or scan the pictures. You have all of them."

She snatched the envelope and hugged it to her chest. "I don't believe you."

Frustration and desperation built inside him. "Phoebe, last week I gave you the only printed copy of the photo in the paper. I didn't leak it. That means either you did or someone has access to wherever you kept it."

Doubt clouded her eyes and then she shook her head. "That's impossible. You're trying to divert the blame. I'm warning you, Carter, if any more pictures become public, I will see you in court. We have nothing more to say to one another."

She yanked open the door, stormed out and raced up the stairs. Carter tried to follow, but the senator, the attorney and a couple of beefy men in dark suits blocked his path. Bodyguards, Carter guessed, judging by the firearm bulges beneath their coats.

How much had they overheard?

"Is Jones telling the truth?" Phoebe's grandfather asked from her bedroom doorway.

Phoebe pressed her fingertips to her throbbing temple and stared out her bedroom window. "He can't be. I had the picture in my nightstand drawer. No one had access to it except

Mildred, and she's like family. She'd never do something like this. Carter has to have sent the picture to the paper."

He joined her on the window seat and took her hand. For the first time Phoebe noticed the blue veins beneath his parchment-like skin. She'd never seen him look this tired or defeated. "I meant, is he telling the truth about you being unhappy in Washington."

Phoebe cringed and met his troubled gaze. "You were eavesdropping."

"Roger thought it best in case Jones made threats."

The attorney. He'd grilled Phoebe this morning when she'd returned from Carter's, trying to determine what, if any, case they had against Carter. It saddened Phoebe to think a private relationship could become a public legal battle.

As the senator's speech writer, Phoebe had become very good at deflecting attention to less troublesome topics. She laced her fingers through his and called upon all her skill. "After grandmother died, you seemed lost and so was I. No one forced me to transfer from UNC to Georgetown, and no one made me pursue a government degree. I made those choices because I wanted to help.

"Being your speech writer and hostess is an exciting job. I get to meet people and travel to places I would never get to see in any other career. I have no regrets about working for you, and spending time with you is an added bonus. Granddad, you're all the family I have left. I love you, and I support your political career wholeheartedly. I will be there for you as long as you need me."

"But this is not the life you had pictured for yourself when you were dating Jones," he countered accurately.

"I was so young and, like Mom, I hadn't finished school. I knew you wouldn't approve, so I hid my relationship with Carter, and that hurt him. When I introduced him to you as a classmate he thought I was ashamed of him, ashamed of our love, and he dumped me. The day you met him is the last day I saw him until two weeks ago when I sought him out to get back our pictures. Evidently he's held a grudge all these years and has finally found a way to settle it."

"Do you still love him?"

Yes, even though he'd hurt her, but she held her confession deep inside. "That was a long time ago and even if I were falling for him all over again, it's a moot point now. I could never trust a man who'd betray me."

"And this man you fell in love with *twice,* is he the type to deliberately hurt the woman he loves?"

She should have known he'd see right through her political spin and immediately zero in on the weakest part of her argument. "Who else could it be?"

"I don't know, but we'll find out." He rose stiffly and crossed the room. He stopped in the doorway. Sadness and regret deepened the lines on his face. "One thing we Lancasters have in common, Phoebe, is the courage to pursue our passions regardless of the obstructions we might encounter. My passion was politics. Your mother's was her love for your father. Unfortunately, *I* was Gracie's obstacle. I hate obstacles. I hate being one even more."

With that he turned on his heel and left Phoebe staring after him. Questions tumbled through her mind. What did he mean? Had she lost him? Was he calling her a coward for not having the courage to tell the truth twelve years ago? If so, he didn't have to. She could do that all by herself.

"Senator Lancaster to see you, Carter," Jes said over the intercom.

Carter's gut clenched and his pulse accelerated. He shoved the contract on which he'd been trying to concentrate into a file folder. In the three days since the story had broken, the senator's team had dismissed the picture as a youthful indiscretion. When contacted by reporters, Carter had refused to comment. He'd hoped to hear from the Lancaster household, but from Phoebe not her grandfather. Losing her this time hurt twice as much as the last time, because he knew she wasn't happy. Because she believed he'd betrayed her. Because he loved her more now than before.

"Show him in." Carter rose and waited behind his walnut desk. He was proud of his professionally decorated office and the original art on the walls. His workspace was a visible testament to his success and how far he'd come.

The senator barely glanced at the furnishings. He tossed a sheaf of papers onto Carter's desk and fixed his narrowed eyes on Carter's face. "Your father is Lieutenant General Victor Jones."

What did his father have to do with anything? "Yes, sir."

"He consulted with the Defense Committee last year. Smart man. Good Marine. I called him yesterday. He says you're military trained, the best damned computer forensics man in the country, and that the corps was sorry to lose you. Vic assures me that you have too much integrity to pull a stunt like this."

His comments rendered Carter speechless—a rare event. His father had never expressed anything remotely like pride in Carter's accomplishments. Carter's medical discharge from the Marines had been a disappointment to the old man, and he'd further angered his father when he'd rejected a pitying offer to *help him find a place.*

"The pictures were submitted electronically to the newspapers," the senator continued. "If you're half as good as your father says you are at tracking computer transactions, then bring me the man who hurt my granddaughter."

Did that mean the senator no longer suspected him? What did Phoebe think? "What purpose will that serve, Senator? The press has already let it go."

"If I have a traitor in my camp, then I want to know who it is. I'll pay double your usual rate."

A traitor. Anger rose swiftly inside Carter. If someone had hurt Phoebe, he'd nail the sorry bastard. "I don't want your money, sir. I want the person who did this as much as you do."

"And now you have my contacts at the papers and the full cooperation of my entire staff at your disposal to aid in your search. My private number is on the top page. Use it when you have something to report." Lancaster headed for the door, but he paused. "You look like hell, Jones, and so does Phoebe. Fix this."

The door closed behind him. Adrenaline raced through Carter's veins. The senator had just given him a mission—one Carter knew he could complete.

But would it make a difference? Was it too late?

"My carrot cake is going to fall if you don't wipe that miserable expression off your face," Mildred chastised Phoebe over breakfast Friday morning.

"Sorry." Phoebe forced a smile.

Mildred made a disgusted sound and stirred the softened block of cream cheese in her bowl.

Phoebe had never been able to fool the housekeeper. She couldn't believe Mildred had leaked the photo…any more than she could believe Carter had. She'd seen the truth in his eyes even though she'd tried to deny it. During the past four days Phoebe had struggled to hold on to her anger and her sense of betrayal, but her grandfather's words pricked her conscience. Would a man she'd fallen in love with twice deceive her? Her judgment couldn't possibly be that faulty. Could it?

Twelve years ago Carter had accepted Phoebe unconditionally *despite* her being a famous politician's granddaughter not *because* of her powerful connections. He'd even refused payment for tutoring her in computer science once they'd started dating. She'd been a loner and he'd taken her into his circle of friends. She hadn't known how to have fun, and he'd taught her. Not once had he deliberately hurt her. In fact, he'd gone out of his way to make her happy. Even his recent insistence that she tell her grandfather about her dissatisfaction with life in D.C. had been for her own good.

But she'd hurt him and insulted his pride. Twice. Was that something a man could ever forget?

She finally admitted what her heart had known all along. Carter hadn't released the picture. But if he hadn't, then who had? Who stood to gain by driving a wedge between her grandfather and herself? She reviewed and edited the mental list she'd made on the drive to Carter's until only one name remained.

Phoebe exhaled slowly. Guilt made her stomach churn. She'd accused the wrong man once before. If she did so a second time, she ran the risk of her grandfather never trusting her advice again, and her revelation would bring a fresh round of scandal to his campaign—one that could end his presidential bid. Either way, she'd lose.

"You could always call him," Mildred broke into Phoebe's ruminations.

"Who?"

Mildred tsked and turned back to her mixing bowl. "You know who."

Carter. She wanted to beg him to give her another chance. Would he slam the door in her face? "No. I need to apologize and groveling should be done in person."

"Then you can talk to him this morning. He has an eleven o'clock appointment with the senator."

Her heart missed a beat. "Mildred, did anyone come to the house while Granddad and I were out of town?"

"The yes-man came by on Friday afternoon to pick up some papers for your grandfather. Said it was something you'd forgotten." She didn't bother to hide her contempt for her least favorite of the senator's employees. "I was busy with the water heater repairman, so I let him go about his business."

Her words confirmed Phoebe's suspicions. "Thanks, Mildred. I'd better get ready for the meeting."

Eleven

Fury burned in Carter's stomach. He had a name, now he wanted the man's head.

Mildred showed him into the senator's study. Lancaster rose from behind his desk. "You have proof?"

"Yes, sir. It's—"

"Not yet," he interrupted. "We'll wait for the others to join us."

Frustrated by the delay, Carter glanced at his watch. He and the senator needed to talk about Phoebe. Now was as good a time as any. He reached into his suit pocket, withdrew a stack of photographs and spread them across the leather blotter. Three dozen of Phoebe's smiles beamed up at them like individual rays of sunshine.

"Senator, I'm not politically connected, and I've never set foot inside a country club. I may not be the man you would have chosen for your granddaughter, but I can make Phoebe happy. I don't stand a chance of doing that without your blessing."

Lancaster studied the pictures with a thoughtful expression on his face. "These are from her semester at the University of North Carolina."

"Most of them are. Some are from her first semester at Georgetown. These are from last week." Carter indicated the most recent photos. The senator immediately picked up Carter's favorite. Their last night in Atlanta had been scorching hot. Phoebe had removed her sandals and lifted the hem of her dress to walk in the shallow fountain outside the theater. Seconds before she'd kicked water all over him, Carter had caught an impish grin on her face that had reminded him so much of the past he'd enlarged the image and hung it above his headboard.

Lancaster met his gaze. "You could be right, Jones. But that's Phoebe's decision and until she resigns, her job is in Washington."

"I'm working on that, sir, and no offense, but I have every intention of stealing your most loyal employee."

The senator scooped up the photos and put them in his desk drawer. "You're welcome to try."

Carter nodded acknowledgment of the challenge.

A knock on the door preceded Phoebe's entrance. She looked as edible as cotton candy in a soft yellow dress that skimmed her curves. Her hair hung in a dark gleaming curtain over her shoulders, and her tentative smile filled Carter with heat and hope. As soon as he gave his report, she'd know he hadn't betrayed her. Would the facts and his love be enough to convince her to stay in North Carolina and build a life with him here?

"Jones." The senator's authoritative voice jerked his attention away from Phoebe. "I don't believe you've met my assistant. Daniel Wisenaut. Daniel, Carter Jones."

Had this pretty-boy jackass been Phoebe's lover? Jealousy

ignited in Carter's chest. He fought the fury building inside him and crushed the handle of his briefcase in his left hand when he'd rather break the bones in Phoebe's ex-fiancé's hand instead of shaking politely as courtesy dictated.

"Sit down." Lancaster gestured for Carter to take a seat on the leather sofa beside Phoebe while he and Wisenaut took the club chairs on the opposite side of the coffee table. "I asked Mr. Jones to do a little digging into the photo debacle," he explained to the other two before turning back to Carter. "And what did you find?"

Carter noted Wisenaut's discomfort and opened his briefcase. "Very few Internet crimes are perpetrated by professionals. Most are committed by amateurs who aren't smart enough to cover their tracks. This one was particularly easy to solve." He laid a copy of the e-mail on the table between them. He'd highlighted the sender's address. "The photo was scanned and electronically submitted to newspapers via e-mail. This is one of your personal e-mail addresses, isn't it, Wisenaut?"

The assistant paled. "I didn't send that e-mail. Somebody set me up. I would never do anything to damage the senator's campaign."

Carter ground his molars and restrained an urge to plant his fist in Wisenaut's lying mouth. "But you would do something to hurt Phoebe. Like telling the senator she was gay to avoid blame for the broken engagement when she discovered you were using her as a gravy train to the White House or sullying her reputation so that her grandfather wouldn't rely on her counsel."

"Why are you trying to pin this on me? If the senator's presidential bid fails, I'm out of a job."

"My sources say otherwise. You were blackening Phoebe's name so the senator would endorse *you* to take his place in the senate instead of Phoebe." Carter laid a second document on the table. "You really should learn to shut down your computer when you're not using it or at least install a firewall. I was able to access your files in a matter of minutes. I found this letter asking for financial support for an upcoming senatorial campaign on your hard drive."

Wisenaut wisely remained silent.

The senator looked downright dangerous when he was furious. "This is outrageous."

Carter tossed another stack of papers on the table. "Here's the database he had connected to the solicitation letter. The file name is Loyal Contributor's List, Senator."

"Roger," the senator bellowed. "Get in here."

The attorney stormed in instantly. He'd obviously been waiting outside the door for the summons.

"Daniel is our leak," Lancaster informed him.

"No, Senator," Wisenaut protested. "I've been a loyal employee for years. You can't trust him. He took pornographic pictures of your granddaughter. Besides, I was with you at the beach."

"I believe Carter." Phoebe's quiet comment caught everyone's attention—especially Carter's. She met his gaze and the trust he found in her eyes humbled him. "Daniel told Granddad he was ill and left the beach early Friday morning. Mildred said Daniel came here on Friday afternoon to pick up a document I'd forgotten. Granddad, I e-mailed you the special interest file from Atlanta on Thursday night—the night Daniel discovered I was with Carter. There was no missing document. And Daniel had freedom of the house because Mildred was tied up with a repairman. I don't know what he was looking for, but he found what he must have believed to be pay dirt if his goal was, as Carter said, to blacken my name."

Carter covered Phoebe's hand. "Do you still have the photo?"

Her fingers laced through his and hope swelled in his chest. "It's in my nightstand drawer. I checked as soon as we returned from Atlanta."

"You think his prints are on it?"

The attorney stepped forward. "That's the first thing I'll have the police check."

Daniel bolted to his feet. "This is entrapment."

"Not really," Roger corrected. "Entrapment is—"

"Hold it, Roger." The senator offered Carter his hand. "Thank you, Mr. Jones. I believe you and Phoebe have a few things to straighten out. Roger and I will clean up this mess."

A clear dismissal. Carter collected his briefcase and followed Phoebe out of the study.

"Phoebe—"

"Carter—"

They spoke simultaneously. Phoebe pressed one hand to her agitated stomach and held up the other. "Me first. I need to grovel. But not here."

A smile curved Carter's lips and lit his eyes. "Then where?"

"Follow me." She led him out the back door, across the patio surrounding the swimming pool and into the shade of the guest cottage. Her nerves fluttered like a flock of startled pigeons as soon as she closed and locked the door behind him. The words she'd rehearsed this morning while dressing for the meeting evaporated. Where was a teleprompter when you needed one? She knotted her fingers. "This used to be my favorite hiding place."

"When you were a girl?" He glanced around the room. His gaze lingered on the stairs leading to the loft bedroom before returning to hers.

"Yes."

"Did you need to hide often?" The soft concern in his eyes melted her.

"Only when my parents argued with each other or with Granddad."

"There were a lot of arguments?"

"Yes, they were strong-minded people and each said hurtful things they couldn't take back. And as I told you before, after the last fight, my parents left and didn't return. So…I've always hated arguments and confrontations. That's one of the reasons I didn't fight for you twelve years ago. I was afraid I'd say the wrong thing and drive you away, so I said nothing and I lost you, anyway." She had to look away from the understanding on his face or she'd start crying and never get this out.

"Phoebe—"

"I'm not finished," she interrupted.

He gestured for her to continue.

"My fear of arguments is probably why I write speeches now. I can go over and over the words until I'm sure they sound right and can't be misinterpreted." The lump in her throat refused to be dislodged and her eyes stung. "I've always made it a practice to never say things I'd regret, but I've said hateful things to you, Carter, and I wish I could take them back."

He closed the distance between them and gently wiped a tear from her cheek with his fingertips. "You didn't say anything you didn't have a right to say. Operation Seduction *was* a deliberate attempt to get you into bed."

Pain slammed her.

He pressed his fingers over her lips. "Let me tell you why."

He flicked open the top button on her dress. His whisper-light touch against her neck and collarbone quickened Phoebe's breath. "I wanted to settle down. I wanted a family, roots and all the things we talked about twelve years ago." The second button opened. "That's why I bought the house. Sawyer and Rick and I made our own family—an unofficial brotherhood."

His actions made it difficult to concentrate on his words.

She pressed her hands over his, stilling his fingers. "What are you doing?"

His smile dimpled his cheeks and crinkled the skin at the corners of his eyes. "Helping you grovel. I'd prefer you do it naked."

Her teeth dug into her bottom lip as she tried not to laugh. She lowered her hands. "You're doing it again."

"What?"

"Distracting me from my troubles. It's something you did twelve years ago. Sometimes…sometimes being with you was all that kept me sane."

"Want me to stop?"

"No, I just want you to know that I'm aware of what you're doing and that I appreciate it. I always have. I'm sorry I interrupted. Carry on, please."

"I could never find a woman I could picture sharing my home with…except for you, Phoebe. And that really ticked me off." He swiftly unfastened the next three buttons and then eased her dress over her shoulders. It floated to the floor.

Phoebe stood self-consciously in front of him clad in the only fancy lingerie set she owned—a lacy and almost-sheer yellow set that she'd bought specifically to go with this linen dress but had never worn because it was just so…so not her.

His swiftly indrawn breath and the hunger in his eyes were her reward. "You're even more beautiful now than before. Remind me to make you grovel more often." He blinked and shook his head. "Now, where was I?"

He traced his fingers beneath her bra straps, over the tops of her breasts and then reached behind her to flick open the clasp. Phoebe shivered as he pulled the fabric away. "When you came back and wanted to destroy the pictures and erase our past, I wanted to punish you for being able to forget."

"I…never…forgot." Her words came out jerkily as he skimmed her panties down her legs.

He straightened and Phoebe reveled in the jealousy in his face. "You were going to marry Wisenaut."

She grimaced, hating that she'd been so stupid, but thankful that she'd been wise enough to call off the engagement. "I felt guilty because I didn't want to run for office. I guess I saw Daniel as a consolation prize for Granddad—someone who loved politics as much as he did. But I had no idea Daniel was so eager to run for office or that he'd use dirty tricks to get there."

Phoebe realized Carter had stripped her bare while he remained completely dressed. That wouldn't do. She tackled his shirt buttons, pausing to stroke the warm skin beneath. Once his shirt was completely unfastened she shoved it, along with his jacket, off his shoulders.

The wiry curls on his chest tickled her palms. "When Lily and Lynn showed me your photo album, I was devastated. There wasn't one single picture of me in it. I was convinced you'd already forgotten all about me and that hurt. Only the fact that you still had our private pictures gave me hope maybe you hadn't totally erased our past from your memory."

He kicked off his shoes, revealing bare feet. Did the man never wear socks? And then he cupped her breasts, stroking the tight tips with his thumbs. Phoebe closed her eyes and clenched her teeth on a moan.

Carter's lips touched her throat. "When Sawyer and Rick married, I became the odd man out. The fifth wheel. The spare tire. When you showed up on my patio, I convinced myself that I had exaggerated the memories of us and that all I had to do was to sleep with you one more time to get you out of my system. That's where Operation Seduction came into play." His fingers brushed her cheek.

Phoebe lifted her lids and lost herself in the honesty and

the hunger in his eyes. "I was wrong, Phoebe. Making love with you was better than before. And once wasn't enough." He cupped her face in both hands.

"I'll never get enough," he whispered against her lips. "Of your lips. Your skin. Your taste." He sipped from her collarbone, her nipple. His fingers found the dampness between her legs and stroked her with unnerving accuracy.

Phoebe's pulse raced and her legs trembled. She couldn't catch her breath. She reached between them to tackle his belt buckle, but he pulled back and captured her hands. "If you expect coherent sentences from me, you're going to have to leave that job to me."

She smiled, hugging the knowledge to herself that she affected him as strongly as he did her.

"Does your hideout have a bed?"

She threaded her fingers through his and led him up the stairs, not stopping until they stood beside the big canopy bed. As a child she'd climbed in and closed the curtains, hiding herself away from the arguments.

He swiftly stripped off his pants and briefs. "I keep your pictures in a hidden compartment."

Phoebe's lungs swelled as she inhaled the scent of his arousal. Her nipples tightened, aching for him to touch her again.

As if he'd read her mind, Carter fused the heat of his body to hers from chest to knee. His ravenous kiss rocked her equilibrium. His bare thigh pressed between her legs, nudging the most sensitive part of her, and his hard, hot flesh scorched her stomach. His fingers spread over her bottom, cupping her and pulling her closer still. But it wasn't close enough. She needed him inside.

Desire suffused her and she clung tightly to him, afraid to let go and lose him again. She tangled her tongue with his, hooked her calf behind his knee and raked her nails down his back. He shivered just as he'd always done when she teased the small of his back.

His hands scraped over her, urgently shaping her waist, hips, breasts and every pleasure point in between. Holding him, kissing him, loving him, fused her past, her present and her future, filling her with so much emotion she couldn't contain it. This was right. This was love. She wouldn't turn her back on it again.

Carter tumbled her onto the bed and quickly rolled on top of her. He pinned her to the mattress with his weight and Phoebe couldn't imagine a place she'd rather be than here in his arms with his thighs between hers. She urged him closer, but he resisted her urgent tugs.

His hands and lips burned a trail over her skin from her breasts to her navel and below. He stroked her with his tongue, finding the one spot guaranteed to drive her wild. She ached for him, but she didn't want to climax alone. She cupped his chin and lifted his lips from her body.

"Carter, please, I need you here." She showed him where.

His sapphire eyes locked with hers. "Whatever you say, sugar."

He rose, pausing long enough to retrieve protection from his pants, and then he moved over her and filled her in one deep, solid stroke. His lips seared hers, catching her gasps, her moans. Phoebe molded his muscles, stroked his supple skin and relished his musky scent.

She forced her heavy lids open and caught his face in her hands. Their eyes met. She arched into his thrusts and looked deep into the eyes of the man she loved as release rocked her. He shuddered, thrust deeper and called her name.

Carter collapsed to his elbows. For several moments the only sounds Phoebe heard were her pulse pounding in her ears and their panting breaths, and then Carter rolled onto his side and pulled her with him. He tucked her head against his shoulder and held her close—the way he used to. His fingers combed the tangles from her hair.

She spread her palm over his heart, feeling its rhythm slow as hers did. Why couldn't they lock the real world out and stay here forever? She traced a finger over the tattoo. "Explain this?"

"A souvenir from my first furlough. Know anything about the history of barbed wire?"

Phoebe shook her head.

"When barbed wire was first invented it completely changed life in the American West. Depending on your point of view, it was either a blessing or a curse. Some called it the Devil's Rope because your first encounter with it was likely to be painful. Like love. A blessing. A curse. Life-changing."

She pressed a kiss to his chest. "I'm sorry."

"So am I. I wish I'd had the guts to fight for you, but I didn't because I always thought you were too good for me. I didn't come here to seduce you today." His words rumbled beneath her ear. Phoebe rose up on her elbow to meet his gaze. Emotion darkened his eyes and his jaw muscles bunched. "I love you, Phoebe. I want to marry you, to have a family with you the way we'd once planned. I want more than this." He gestured to encompass the guest cottage.

Happiness expanded within her, forcing her doubts to retreat another step. "I want more than stolen moments, too."

"What about your grandfather?"

Phoebe sighed. "I'd like to see him through the election, but I'll understand if you don't want me to."

His nostrils flared as he inhaled deeply. He rolled onto his side and hooked his thigh over hers. He brushed the hair off her cheek with gentle fingers. "I always thought a woman had to be like my mother—willing to follow her husband's career wherever it took them. But who packs their bags isn't important. Being together is, and if you want to stay with your grandfather, then I'll relocate CyberSniper to the D.C. area."

"You'd leave Sawyer and Rick?"

He shrugged. "It's only a five-hour drive. We can keep track by phone and e-mail."

That he'd sacrifice his adopted family for her touched her deeply. "No, Carter, you're right. I'm not happy in Washington. When we go back inside, I'll tell my grandfather that I can't be his hostess and speech writer any longer."

She caught his hand and pressed it to her cheek. "I love you and I hurt you by not trusting you now and twelve years ago. I'm sorry."

"We both made mistakes." He brushed his lips over her forehead. "Phoebe, I can't promise we'll never argue, but I can promise that I'll never willingly leave you again."

"And I promise to always be honest with you even if I'm afraid I won't like your response. I can't live my life in fear of saying the wrong thing."

"Then, sugar, we need to get married, and I know just the place. After we tell the senator, I'll call Sam."

"Deal."

The activity around the house alerted Phoebe that something wasn't right. Had the police come for Daniel? Had something happened to her grandfather? She'd left her cell phone in the house. Had anyone known where to find her?

She hurried inside with Carter right beside her. Mildred bustled around the kitchen, fixing what looked like trays of hors d'oeuvres. "Thank goodness you're here. The press conference is due to start in a few minutes. He's holding it on the front porch. Everything's already set up. Go." She shooed them out of the kitchen.

Phoebe's heart slowed marginally. A press conference meant her grandfather was all right. She headed for the entrance. She found him in the foyer. The sounds of the press setting up outside penetrated the front door.

"Granddad, is everything okay?"

His gaze went from Phoebe to Carter beside her and back. "I believe so."

Certain he knew exactly what she'd been doing in the guest house for the past hour, Phoebe's cheeks caught fire. She wiped her damp palms on her dress and realized when she licked her dry lips that all traces of her lipstick had been kissed away. "Can I speak with you a moment?"

"Five minutes, Senator," one of the staffers said.

"In my office."

Phoebe took a deep breath and glanced at Carter. His encouraging nod and the love in his eyes gave her courage. She motioned for him to wait in the foyer and followed her grandfather into the study. Taking a bracing breath, Phoebe closed the door behind them. "I don't know how to say this."

"Stop editing the words in your head, Phoebe, and tell me what's in your heart." He knew her too well.

She fixed her eyes on her grandfather's lined face, willing him to understand. "I love you, and I am proud to be your granddaughter." She took another deep breath. "But I'm in love with Carter, and I want to marry him and have a family with him *here* in North Carolina."

He didn't look surprised. In fact, he didn't look anything. He wore his poker face. That in itself tied her intestines into knots. "What about your job? The campaign?"

Even his voice seemed devoid of emotion. She loved him so much, owed him so much, but her next words could be the final straw.

"I'll do anything I can to support you from here, but I

don't want to lose Carter again. I don't want to lose you, either, but I can't be two places at once. And I..."

Phoebe studied her knotted fingers, bracing herself for his anger and trying to find a last speck of bravery. She lifted her gaze. "I don't want to run for your vacated senate seat. I'm not cut out to be a politician. I'm sorry."

A knock on the door startled Phoebe. "Two minutes, sir."

"Phoebe, this family has made innumerable sacrifices for my career. I lost your mother because I made her choose between the man she loved and my plans for her. I may be an old man, but I hope I'm a little wiser now than I was then."

Another rap on the door made her jump. Usually she was the one watching the clock to make sure the senator didn't keep the press waiting, but today she could only watch his face for signs that she'd disappointed him—signs she didn't see.

He looped his arm around her shoulders and guided her toward the door, but paused with his hand on the knob. "Is he going to make an honest woman out of you or am I going to have to take him out back and teach him a lesson?"

His teasing comment meant he didn't hate her. Tension drained from her muscles and a smile trembled on her lips. "We're going to get married."

"That's all I needed to know." He opened the door. The front door already stood open, waiting for him to step out onto the brick semicircular porch where he had made so many of his other announcements. He pointed to Carter as he crossed the foyer. "Join us outside, Jones."

Her grandfather stepped behind the microphone someone had set up at the top of the stairs. Phoebe took her usual spot just behind her grandfather's right shoulder. Nervously she reached for Carter's hand and met his gaze.

"Okay?" he whispered, and laced his fingers through hers.

Was everything going to work out? Her grandfather hadn't

exactly given his blessing, but he hadn't ordered her to leave, either. "I think so."

"Ladies and gentlemen," her grandfather's voice interrupted. "I've served my country for thirty-five years, and as many of you know, my supporters have been urging me to run for president in the upcoming election." He paused and Phoebe smiled. Her grandfather was the master of pregnant pauses. He used them deliberately to build suspense.

When the press quit fidgeting, he continued. "But I think the time has come for me to rest on my laurels—I have quite a few of those, you know—and let one of the young guns take over."

Phoebe listened in stunned silence. Cameras whirred furiously. She snapped her gaping mouth closed.

"I want to spend time with my family, attend my granddaughter's wedding to this fine gentleman, Carter Jones. And, God willing, I'm going to spoil a few great-grandkids absolutely rotten."

He waited for the laughter to die down. "Now, do you have any questions for me or do you want to quiz Phoebe on the wedding details? I'm rather anxious to hear those myself."

As the reporters snickered, the senator stepped away from the microphone and took Phoebe into his arms. "I'm proud of you for finding the courage to follow your heart. Be happy, sweet pea. Be happy."

Tears streamed over Phoebe's cheeks and into the corners of her smile. "I already am."

He clapped Carter on the shoulder. "Jones, take care of my girl or you'll answer to me."

"Yes, sir. I'll do my best."

* * * * *

Bronwyn Jameson

will take you away with her breathtaking new miniseries,

PRINCES OF THE OUTBACK

Beginning with

THE RUGGED LONER

Silhouette Desire #1666
Available July 2005

When Angelina Mori returned for the funeral of Tomas Carlisle's father, offering hugs and tears, Tomas hadn't felt comforted. He'd dragged in air rich with her perfume, felt her curves against his body and set aside this woman who no longer felt as a childhood friend should. She smelled different, she looked different and right now, in the dark, he swore she was looking at him differently, too....

Meet the other Carlisle brothers!
THE RICH STRANGER, available September 2005
THE RUTHLESS GROOM, available November 2005

Only from Silhouette Books!

**Welcome to Silhouette Desire's
brand-new installment of**

*The drama unfolds for six of
the state's wealthiest bachelors.*

BLACK-TIE SEDUCTION
by Cindy Gerard
(Silhouette Desire #1665, July 2005)

LESS-THAN-INNOCENT
INVITATION
by Shirley Rogers
(Silhouette Desire #1671, August 2005)

STRICTLY CONFIDENTIAL
ATTRACTION
by Brenda Jackson
(Silhouette Desire #1677, September 2005)

*Look for three more titles from Michelle Celmer,
Sara Orwig and Kristi Gold to follow.*

If you enjoyed what you just read,
then we've got an offer you can't resist!

Take 2 bestselling love stories FREE!
Plus get a FREE surprise gift!

Clip this page and mail it to Silhouette Reader Service™

IN U.S.A.
3010 Walden Ave.
P.O. Box 1867
Buffalo, N.Y. 14240-1867

IN CANADA
P.O. Box 609
Fort Erie, Ontario
L2A 5X3

YES! Please send me 2 free Silhouette Desire® novels and my free surprise gift. After receiving them, if I don't wish to receive anymore, I can return the shipping statement marked cancel. If I don't cancel, I will receive 6 brand-new novels every month, before they're available in stores! In the U.S.A., bill me at the bargain price of $3.80 plus 25¢ shipping and handling per book and applicable sales tax, if any*. In Canada, bill me at the bargain price of $4.47 plus 25¢ shipping and handling per book and applicable taxes**. That's the complete price and a savings of at least 10% off the cover prices—what a great deal! I understand that accepting the 2 free books and gift places me under no obligation ever to buy any books. I can always return a shipment and cancel at any time. Even if I never buy another book from Silhouette, the 2 free books and gift are mine to keep forever.

225 SDN DZ9F
326 SDN DZ9G

Name	(PLEASE PRINT)	
Address	Apt.#	
City	State/Prov.	Zip/Postal Code

Not valid to current Silhouette Desire® subscribers.

Want to try two free books from another series?
Call 1-800-873-8635 or visit www.morefreebooks.com.

* Terms and prices subject to change without notice. Sales tax applicable in N.Y.
** Canadian residents will be charged applicable provincial taxes and GST.
All orders subject to approval. Offer limited to one per household.
® are registered trademarks owned and used by the trademark owner and or its licensee.

DES04R   ©2004 Harlequin Enterprises Limited

HARLEQUIN® *Blaze*™

New York Times bestselling author

Elizabeth Bevarly

answers the question

Can men and women have sex and still be friends?

with

INDECENT SUGGESTION
Blaze #189

Best friends Becca and Turner try hypnosis to kick their smoking habit…instead, they get the uncontrollable urge to burn up the sheets! Doesn't that make them more than friends?

Be sure to catch this funny, sexy story available in July 2005!

Silhouette Desire

**Coming in July 2005
from Silhouette Desire**

DYNASTIES: THE ASHTONS

*A family built on lies...brought together
by dark, passionate secrets.*

Sheri WhiteFeather's

BETRAYED
BIRTHRIGHT

(Silhouette Desire #1663)

When Walker Ashton decided to search for his
past, he found it on a Sioux Nation reservation.
Helping him to deal with his Native American
heritage was Tamra Winter Hawk, a woman who
cherished her roots and had Walker longing
for a future with her. But when his real world
commitments intruded upon their fantasy
liaison, would they find a way to keep the
connection they'd formed?

Available at your favorite retail outlet.

COMING NEXT MONTH

#1663 BETRAYED BIRTHRIGHT—Sheri WhiteFeather
Dynasties: The Ashtons
When Walker Ashton decided to search for his past, he found it on a
Sioux Nation reservation. Helping him to deal with his Native American
heritage was Tamra Winter Hawk, a woman who cherished her roots
and had Walker longing for a future together. But when his real-world
commitments intruded upon their fantasy liaison, would they find a way
to keep the connection they'd formed?

#1664 THE LAST REILLY STANDING—Maureen Child
Three-Way Wager
Aidan Reilly was determined to win the bet he'd made with his brothers.
Three months without sex meant one thing: spend *a lot* of time with his
best gal pal, Terry Evans. She had given up on love long ago because the
pain just wasn't worth it. Then…temptation proved to be too much. The last
Reilly standing had lost the bet, but could he win the girl?

#1665 BLACK-TIE SEDUCTION—Cindy Gerard
Texas Cattleman's Club: The Secret Diary
Millionaire Jacob Thorne got on Christine Travers's last nerve—the sensible
lady had no time for Jacob's flirtatious demeanor. But when the two butted
heads at an auction, Jacob embarked on a black-tie seduction that would
prove she had needs—womanly needs—that only he could satisfy.

#1666 THE RUGGED LONER—Bronwyn Jameson
Princes of the Outback
Australian widower Tomas Carlisle was stunned to learn he had to father
a child to inherit a cattle empire. Making a deal with longtime friend
Angelina Mori seemed the perfect solution—until their passion escalated
and Angelina mounted an all-out attack on Tomas's defense against hot,
passionate, *committed* love.

#1667 CRAVING BEAUTY—Nalini Singh
They'd married within mere days of meeting. Successful tycoon
Marc Bordeaux had been enchanted by Hira Dazirah's desert beauty. But
Hira feared Marc only craved her outer good looks. This forced Marc to
prove his true feelings to his virgin bride—and tender actions spoke louder
than words….

#1668 LIKE LIGHTNING—Charlene Sands
Although veterinarian Maddie Brooks convinced rancher Trey Walker to
allow her to live and work on his ranch, there was no way Trey would ever
romance the sweet and sexy Maddie. He was a victim of the "Walker Curse"
and couldn't commit to any woman. But once they gave in to temptation,
Maddie was determined to make their arrangement more permanent….

SDCNM0605